Dr Maud's PROJECT MUCK

ANN CARTER

Lammas Publishing

*This book is dedicated to my children,
Vivian, Jann, John, Wanda, and David,
with love, always.*

1

Identical twins are often mistaken for one another. Some of us experience telepathic awareness when the other is in trouble too. This happens with my sister Gabriella and me.

Gabriella was a psychiatrist in Norwich before taking early retirement to pursue her enthusiasm for horticulture. She downsized to a small house with a large garden in Bungay, Suffolk where she now applies her analytic skills to the science behind organic gardening. Believe it or not, she has become a locally recognized authority on home composting. Her prize-winning flowers and vegetables are legendary in Suffolk. She even writes an occasional column, 'Muck to Money', in the gardening section of her local newspaper.

Just for the record, I, the elder twin by twenty minutes, have no interest in composting. I employ a gardener to mow my lawn, prune my shrubs and pull my weeds as necessary. He throws the trimmings onto a muck pile at the end of the garden. That is as far as my composting activity goes. I just got dragged into Gabriella's murky mess by being her identical twin.

I was up early on the Monday when it all began. My husband Richard had already left. He needed to catch the 6.10 am car ferry from Dunoon, where we live, and was now *en route* to Glasgow Airport. An early flight would get him to London in time for the start of his conference, which might last up to two weeks.

I was clearing away the remains of our early breakfast. Out of the blue, I felt a strong urge to contact my twin. I hadn't seen much of her since my marriage a year ago, so with Richard away for a couple of weeks, it seemed a good opportunity to go down to Bungay and spend time with her.

One problem contacting Gabriella by phone is that she doesn't always bother to answer. She says that this is the best way to avoid cold calls and advises me to do the same. Serious callers, she asserts, will always leave a message. Fine, except that she doesn't always bother to check her phone for messages either. Therefore, knowing her to be an early riser and knowing too that she checks her email right after breakfast, I emailed her immediately to suggest a visit while Richard was away. In the email I said that if she could meet my train the following day at Beccles station, I would travel by rail rather than drive. Gabriella's house has only a single garage and a narrow driveway, so a second car there can be a nuisance. It's also quite a long drive from Scotland to East Anglia.

The email bounced back.

I knew I hadn't made a mistake with her address because I had simply used the reply function to the email she herself sent to me the previous evening, reminding me to deadhead my roses. Gabriella always was bossy.

I tried to send the email again a second and a third time with the same result, so there was nothing for it but to try the telephone. For once, she answered straight away. She sounded her normal cheerful self.

"Aggie! Good to hear from you! You don't normally telephone. Is something wrong?"

"Nothing wrong here, Gabs, but I should tell you that an email I sent you this morning bounced back. There may be a problem at your end."

"It was working last night," she retorted. "I daresay there's some kind of problem at your end, Aggie. You should have it checked."

"I've already…" I began.

"Just hold a minute while I check mine," she ordered. "I haven't done my email this morning. In fact, I was just about to do it when you called. Hang on."

Didn't I tell you she's bossy?

"Actually Aggie, no email has come in since I sent that one to you to remind you about your roses, not even the usual spam. The screen's also telling me I've no broadband either. I'd better check with my neighbours to see if they're getting theirs. If I'm the only one affected, I'll call my provider. Thanks for telling me about it, Aggie. Bye!"

"Don't ring off!" I managed to catch her before she put the phone down. "The email was to ask whether you'd like me to come and stay with you for a couple of weeks. Richard's away so if you're free it would be a good opportunity to get together again, just the two of us. That's if you're free of course."

"No problem, just come on down."

"Right, see you tomorrow then."

"Great!"

We rang off.

Before leaving for Bungay, I needed to return a couple of library books and visit the cash machine, so it was more than two hours before I remembered I had not asked Gabriella to meet my train at Beccles. I called her again.

Once again Gabriella did pick up the phone but this time there was silence down the line. Where was my sister's usual effusive greeting? Her mobile would tell her who was calling. What on earth was wrong?

"Gabby?" I waited about twenty seconds, but no sound came. "Are you there?"

"Oh, Aggie," Gabriella sounded frightened. "Thank goodness it's you."

"What's wrong Gabby? What's happened? Have you had a fall or something?"

"No, no, nothing like that."

"Are you mobile?"

"Yes."

"Well then, I was calling to ask you to meet my train in at Beccles tomorrow. But maybe you don't feel up to it."

"Well, er, I don't know Aggie." Gabriella's voice sounded unsure, not at all her usual confident tone. Something had obviously upset her since I called her a couple of hours ago.

"Gabs, I can easily get a taxi from Beccles station if there's a problem. Would you prefer that?" There was silence at the other end of the line.

"Gabs," I said, "what's wrong? I thought you wanted me to come. Did I say something to upset you?"

"No Aggie, of course you didn't. Of course I want you to come. It's just that I'm a bit busy. Yes, maybe you should take a taxi."

Something was definitely wrong. She normally wouldn't think twice about driving to meet me.

"Gabs," I said more firmly, "I'm coming on the train tomorrow. Are you planning to meet me in at Beccles? I have to know whether or not I need to book a taxi."

"No Aggie, I can't meet you." This was all very odd. Gabriella drives everywhere, even short distances that she could easily walk. Why on earth couldn't she drive to Beccles?

"Is there some reason you can't drive at the moment, Gabs?" I asked, "Are you ill?"

"No, it's not that. I'm not ill. It's just that I don't have my car right now."

"You don't have your car!" I exclaimed, "Have you been in an accident? Has something happened to your car?"

"No Aggie, it's not that either. I'm not ill and I haven't been in an accident and the car's all right. It's just that I don't have it here."

Something was definitely amiss. This was certainly not my normal cheerful, confident sister. The sooner I got to Bungay the better. I thought quickly.

"Look," I said, "if you don't have your own car at home, then mine won't be in the way. So look, I won't take the train, I'll drive down. In fact, I'll come today, not tomorrow. I can set off within the next half hour and should be with you in eight- or nine-hours' time. Keep something hot for me to eat if I'm late. I can tell something's wrong, but we won't waste time talking about it now. You can tell me when I get there."

"Oh Aggie," she sighed, "thank you, thank you. You really are a wonderful sister."

I couldn't recall Gabriella telling me that I was a wonderful sister before in her entire life. She must really be in trouble. The sooner I got to Bungay the better.

2

I'd already done the library and cash machine run so there was no reason to delay. I packed a small travel bag, just personal things. There's no need to carry much when Gabriella and myself visit each other. We are the same size and can wear each other's clothes. I grabbed a packet of biscuits, some fruit and a few bottles of water and put them in my Mini. Finally, before setting off, I sent a text message to Richard to let him know I was driving to Bungay to visit Gabriella and that I would call him when I arrived.

During the twenty-minute ferry ride from Dunoon across the Clyde estuary to the mainland I thought about Gabriella and me. We grew up in York and went on to medical school together. We only separated when we pursued different career paths. We retired at about the same time, but both stayed in the area that had been home during our working years. Despite that, we were still close.

I am Dr Angelina Maud (retired). After thirty years in a busy GP practice in Glasgow, I retired to a bungalow in Dunoon, a quiet, scenic area on the west coast of Scotland. There I met and married my next-door neighbour, Richard Carter. Richard is a former government intelligence officer and coincidentally an ex-colleague of Gabriella's son, George. Richard is officially retired but still sits on various committees and has to attend meetings from time to time, usually in London. That's where he would be for the next two weeks.

Gabriella had moved from her psychiatric practice in Norwich to Bungay, one of the pretty small towns in East Anglia. She managed to find her perfect bungalow boasting almost an acre of garden. She had always enjoyed gardening. Now finally she was able to throw herself into horticulture full time. I have to say, the results of her hard work have been spectacular. She wins prizes at both local and national flower shows. Not only does she write her gardening column 'Muck to Money', but she has also been featured in national magazines. During the past year her interest has extended from dig, plant and reap, to the scientific aspects of composting. Marked sections of her garden indicate the sites of her various studies. She told me that she has been liaising with a colleague at an agricultural institute near Cambridge on some of these. I don't know any more about it than that but can't help being impressed.

My musings came to an end abruptly with the slight bump of the car ferry landing on the other side at Gourock. My sat nav guided me unerringly to the M74 south and on to the M6. At Penrith I took the A66 across the Pennines to the A1(M). At Newark on Trent, I branched onto the A17 to King's Lynn, then the A47 to Norwich and on to Bungay on the A146. Luckily, the roads were relatively quiet, so I made good time and reached Bungay by early evening.

I was far too anxious to feel tired on the journey but as soon as I reached Gabriella's bungalow, exhaustion hit, and I was ready to lie down and close my eyes. However, one look at my sister brought the adrenaline rushing back.

Gabriella must have been watching for my arrival because the door opened even as I turned into the driveway. She looked absolutely haggard. She burst into tears, threw her arms around my neck and sobbed for several minutes.

"Aggie, I just don't know what to do," she gasped.

I led her gently to a chair in the kitchen, normally a warm, cosy and cluttered room. That day it was cold and bare. Where were the bits of gardening paraphernalia that usually littered the counters? Where were the empty plant pots, seed packets and magazines? Where was the little laptop computer that should be sitting at the end of the kitchen table?

"I think we'd better have a cup of tea," I said, looking round for the kettle and teapot. "Where's the kettle?"

Gabriella pointed a weak finger towards the sink.

I found the electric kettle in the cupboard under the sink and reconnected it. I looked in the usual cupboard for tea bags, half expecting it to be empty. To my relief, everything looked normal inside, other than the teapot being in the cupboard too. I flipped open other cupboard doors. All contents appeared present and correct as far as I could tell. Hmm! I made the tea, found milk in the refrigerator and brandy in the usual cupboard. I poured us both a cup of strong tea laced with a generous slug of brandy, then sat on a kitchen stool, watching my sister carefully while we sipped. Whether due to the brandy, to my presence, or to both, she became a bit more relaxed.

"What's going on?" I asked, pouring another generous splash of brandy into her second cup of tea, "The kitchen looks bare, and you've stashed everything away in cupboards. Why was the kettle under the sink instead of on the counter and the teapot in the cupboard with the tea bags?"

"I didn't want them to take anything else away."

"Gabs, who are 'they' and what have they taken away?"

"I don't know who they are."

"Well, did you see them?"

"Yes."

"And?"

"They were wearing balaclavas on their heads so I couldn't see their faces."

"Who were?"

"Two men."

"Two men. Do you remember anything else about them?"

"They were wearing all black. The balaclavas were black too."

"Anything else? Tall, short, fat, thin, teenage?"

"Both tallish, slim, and I'd guess older than teenage."

"Did they say anything?"

"One of them told me to stay where I was. Then the other one stood beside me to make sure I stayed there."

"Where did you have to stay? Where were you when the two men came?"

"I was out in the front garden, dead-heading the roses, just like I reminded you to do."

"Well then, you must have seen them arrive. What kind of car did they come in?"

"They left it on the road outside, but it was a jeep of some kind."

"So, let me get this right, Gabs. Two men parked a jeep on the road outside this house, walked down the driveway, saw you among the roses in the front garden and told you to stay where you were. Right so far?"

"Yes."

"They were both slim and tall. They were dressed in black and wearing balaclavas."

"Yes."

"One of them stayed outside with you. Did the other go into the house?"

"Yes."

"Then what happened?"

"He came out carrying one of my computers, the laptop from the kitchen. He took it to the jeep, then came back and waved to the man who was watching me and then they drove off."

"When did this happen?"

"Just after you called this morning to say you were coming."

"I must have called around six-thirty. Was it just after then?"

"Yes."

"Have you reported all this to the police?"

"Yes."

"And what did the police say?"

"They thought it was probably teenagers looking for small items they could sell. They said they would put out an alert for the two men and let me know if they catch them. They weren't optimistic though."

"Did the man that went into the house take anything else besides your laptop?"

"I don't think so. He was in and out of the house very quickly. I don't think he had time to look around. I think he was only after my laptop."

"Did you look carefully when you went back into the house?"

"Yes, of course I did, Aggie, I looked before calling the police. I'm not stupid you know!"

"Well, they may not have taken anything else from the house, Gabs, but what about your car? If they went off in the jeep with your laptop, did they come back later for your car? Or did someone else drive your car away?"

"No Aggie, you've got it wrong. They didn't take my car. Nobody took my car. The car's alright."

Just what was going on? I knew that Gabriella only uses the old laptop in her kitchen for gardening notes, email, calendar, shopping lists and the like. She does all her official stuff, banking, writing, preparing lectures etc., on a much newer desktop model in the bedroom she uses as an office. The old laptop couldn't have been much of a loss and she told me her car was alright, so why was she still so shaken up. The robbery happened hours ago, and the police had assured her they would be looking out for the thieves.

"Gabbie," I said, "when I called you the second time this morning to ask if you would meet my train in at Beccles, you told me you didn't have your car any longer. That's why I drove here. Not that I minded of course," I added hastily, "the traffic was light, and I had an easy drive down. But tell me, have you decided not to drive anymore? I know your eyes aren't as good as they used to be."

That got a reaction, as I expected.

"Don't be so stupid Aggie! There's nothing wrong with my eyesight! It's probably a lot better than yours! Of course I haven't given up driving. I'd just driven it to the garden centre when you called back."

Weird!

"Why did you go to the garden centre after the robbery?"

"I took my car to the garden centre and asked them if I could leave it there for a few days. They know me well and said I could put it in the staff car park. It's behind the garden centre and has a separate entrance and a gate that gets locked up at night. You can't see it from the road. The garden centre staff probably thought I wanted the car to be safe while I was away for a few days. I didn't tell them otherwise. I'd just got home when you called me the second time."

Things were becoming a little clearer. Presumably Gabriella was worried that her car, a bright red late model Audi, would be stolen too. She had hidden it away in the garden centre staff car park. That explained why she was without wheels. But there was still the odd state of her kitchen when I arrived.

"Gabs," I said, "I understand now about your car, but why did you clear everything away in the kitchen."

"I was worried sick. I just cleared up the kitchen for something to do."

"Now let's think this through," I said reasonably. "Two men in black balaclavas arrived in a jeep. One kept you out in the garden while the other pinched your old laptop. High drama like that belongs on television, Gabs, not in a Bungay garden before seven in the morning. It just doesn't make sense."

"Yes, I'm afraid it does. I realised right after talking to the policeman. They were after my compost research. They stole the laptop thinking that's where they'd find all my records. They wouldn't know I do my research work and filing on the desk computer in my office."

"Have you checked to see if the robber went into your office?"

"Yes of course I did! He only went in the kitchen. My office door was locked. I always lock it when I go out of the house."

"Even when you're only out in the garden?"

"Yes, I always lock it routinely. That way I won't ever forget to lock it when I leave the house. You know, Aggie, it won't be long before they find there's nothing important on the laptop."

"Ah, now I understand. That's why you were so worried they might come back."

"Yes, but they won't find anything else if they do. It's all in the car."

I looked round the empty kitchen. "You mean you've put all the papers and gardening stuff that used to be here in the kitchen into your car?"

"Yes, and all the important files out of my office. They're all safe in the car now."

Gabriella had gradually calmed down as the story unfolded, which made it easier for me to link the bits of story into a rational account.

"Yes, now things are becoming much clearer," I said. "You weren't worried about your car being stolen at all. You were worried about your work and papers that were still here in the house. You were worried those two men might come back for them. So, you put everything into your car, then hid your car in a safe place."

"Yes. I do hope they don't know I have the desk computer as well and come back for that."

I thought about all Gabriella had told me. At first glance, it might seem that she had overreacted in her anxiety to protect her horticultural research and discounted the obvious explanation for the theft. As the police suggested, the thieves could just have been looking for things that could be easily sold. On the other hand...

"What about the data on your desk computer Gab? Do you keep copies on storage discs?"

"Oh yes, everything I need is saved on my little plug-in drives and they're all safe in the car now. I've erased all my work from the computer in case they come back again, including an important lecture I'm preparing. That reminds me, can you believe my broadband carrier claims there's nothing wrong and just says I can't have checked my connections properly."

"Did you ask your neighbours if their internet is working?"

"Yes, and I seem to be the only one with a problem. But never mind that for now. What's really worrying me is that the men in balaclavas might be back when they don't find the notes for the lecture I promised to give when I've got a few more results."

"Notes for one of your lectures on plants?"

"Compost actually. It's new information about the effectiveness of different combinations of compost material for use in home gardens. It could have serious implications for the commercial fertilizer market. That's immense you know."

I didn't know, and frankly found the idea that my sister's compost experimentation could seriously impact the commercial fertilizer industry a little wacky. I wondered again if the police view that Gabriella had simply been the victim of petty theft was the correct one.

"Gabs," I spoke carefully, because I didn't want to upset her any further, "if you believe the thieves were only after your lecture notes, just why did you clear everything else out of the kitchen? That was much more than a tidy up. Even the teapot and kettle were stashed away. And also, why does it feel so cold in here?"

"Well, that was what the police advised. They told me not to leave things in full view that might attract petty thieves. They said there have been a lot of reports of petty theft lately. That kettle's brand new and the teapot is Wedgwood."

"Right," I said, forbearing to point out that few people would consider kettles and teapots to be high on a burglar's wish list, "but what about the temperature? Has the heating broken down?"

She thought for a moment.

"Oh Aggie, that's my fault. I switched the electricity off when I was checking the broadband connections. I forgot all about it. Hold on, I'll have it back on in a sec."

Gabriella disappeared into a cupboard leading off the kitchen. She re-emerged, smiling for the first time since I arrived. "There," she said. "The house will soon warm up. I felt a bit cold but just thought we were in for a cold night."

"And I suppose you were turning the electricity off and on again when you were checking why the internet wasn't working. You turned it off but not on again."

"I guess."

"So, you can't have done any cooking today."

"Well, no, I thought you might like to have fish and chips tonight. I'm not hungry."

"When did you last eat?"

"Breakfast I suppose, but really Aggie, I'm not hungry."

"Right," I said, thinking a walk in the fresh air and the seductive aroma from the chippy might change her mind, "let's go and get my dinner while the house is warming up. You'll have to come to show me the way."

I was right.

When we arrived at the chippy, she said, "I'll have some too and eat what I can, and then the birds can have the rest tomorrow morning."

The house was nicely warmed up by the time we got back to eat, and my sister warmed up with each successive mouthful. The birds did not get their treat the next morning.

3

Richard called on Tuesday morning to ask if I'd gone to Bungay since he hadn't heard from me. Poor Richard, in all the rush and confusion I had forgotten to call or email him. Anyway, he said he was glad I had gone, because he might be detained in London a little longer than expected. I apologized for not calling and explained why. I related the story of Gabriella's break-in, how nothing had been taken except her little laptop, and that Gabriella was convinced the thieves had come specifically to steal her research data. Richard was sympathetic because he's quite fond of Gabriella, but thought she was probably overreacting.

"You know, your sister does like to play the drama queen," he said.

"Oh, by the way," I added, "I was forgetting, she lost her internet connection too, although her neighbours haven't lost theirs."

For some reason, that got his attention.

"When did that happen?" he asked.

"Let me ask." I called to the kitchen.

"Gabbie, Richard wants to know when your internet went off. I think it would be best if you talk to him yourself." I put the phone on speaker and took it to her in the kitchen.

I heard Gabriella tell Richard she always takes care of the day's email before she goes to bed. She checks it again after breakfast in case anything important has come in during the night. The internet must have gone off sometime between Sunday evening and Monday morning.

He asked if she had received any unusual emails recently. She said there had been nothing of special interest all week except for one from her colleague Cyril Jenkinson at the Agriculture Institute on Thursday.

Cyril had always taken a friendly interest in her composting, although his main interest was in pollination. In this particular email he asked her to send him details of the chemical breakdown of her recent experiments. He said he was helping his department chief put together a public lecture on home composting.

The request triggered alarm bells for Gabriella. First of all, she couldn't imagine why that degree of technical detail would be appropriate in a lecture to the general public. Second, her work could just possibly have commercial implications. She decided to stall and emailed straight back to say that her data needed more work before it was ready to be shared. She knew that Cyril was well aware of this already, so she assumed her reply would be the end of the matter.

"But then," she told my husband, "this morning my laptop was stolen. It was while I was working in the garden, soon after Aggie called to say she was coming down for a couple of weeks. And Richard," she went on, "I did report it to the police right away but the policeman who came to investigate thought it would probably be teenagers looking for things they could sell. But I don't believe those two men that came to the house in a jeep and came down the drive covered in balaclavas were just petty thieves. One of them stood over me in the garden and made me stay there while the other went into the house and got my laptop. All this at seven in the morning, for heaven's sake!"

"They probably weren't expecting you to be up so early, let alone out in the garden."

"Well, you see, the roses needed deadheading and I wanted to do them before the sun would be hot on my back."

She handed me the phone back. "You tell him the rest Aggie."

"Gabs really was shaken up," I told Richard, "in fact, she bundled all her compost research data into her car and has left it in a safe place. That's why I had to drive here. She hasn't got wheels any longer so she couldn't meet the train."

"Listen," he said, "the police may well be right in thinking this was no more than petty theft, particularly if there have been similar incidents in the neighbourhood recently. However, just in case your sister's right and someone's really after her research, you'd better be alert. Meanwhile, I'll make some enquiries about her internet and try to get it reinstated. Promise to call me immediately if you have any reason to be concerned."

4

After Richard's call, to take Gabriella's mind off the theft of her laptop and its possible implications, I suggested she take a day off from her garden chores and come for a drive out to the coast.

"It's such a lovely day," I told her. "It's a pity to stay indoors. A breath of sea air will do you good."

"There's nothing wrong with the air right here!" she retorted. "I should be out there working in the garden. Gardens don't look after themselves you know. Well," she added, a bit spitefully I thought, "I know yours has to fend for itself but most of us like our gardens to reflect pride of ownership."

I let that one go. Gabriella always did like to feel superior.

"I know you're upset, Gabs," I told her, "but there's no need to be snippy. Richard said to tell him if anything more happens. Let's just the two of us have a day to ourselves and catch up on all the news. We haven't done that for ages. Come on, let's go. You can drive."

"Oh, all right," she conceded, hurrying towards my blue Mini before I changed my mind. She has a mistaken belief that she is the superior driver. "Chances are the villains are still searching through the files on my laptop for the data they're after. I'd guess they'd check through at least a couple of times in case they missed anything. I don't know what they'll do when they realise it isn't there. Thank goodness I did all the work on my desk computer."

"You did say you've taken it off your desk computer, didn't you?" I ventured.

"Of course I did, I told you that yesterday. I copied it onto jump drives, then erased the lot. The jump drives are safe in my car together with the paper files and the car's safe at the garden centre. The frustrating thing is that I can't get at the stuff myself. I suppose we might just as well go off to the coast or wherever else you want to take me."

Gabriella's spirits lifted as we left Bungay. We drove to the coast and strolled companionably along the sand as we had done many times before. But when I suggested lunch in a nearby hotel, Gabriella hesitated. She pointed out that the sun had disappeared behind clouds and maybe that was an appropriate time to leave. There were one or two things she needed to do in the garden. She suggested we go shopping on the way back and have a late lunch at home.

"Lamb chops with new potatoes and broccoli OK with you?" she asked.

I readily agreed.

We walked back to my car and drove back to Gabriella's bungalow via a supermarket. As events turned out though, we didn't get to enjoy our lamb chops until later that evening.

5

"Oh no, not again!" Gabriella screeched as we turned into her driveway. "Aggie, look! The front door is open. Oh Aggs, they must have come back while we were out. What are we going to do?"

Sure enough, the front door was wide open. Gabriella never uses her front door except to answer the doorbell. She keeps it locked and uses the kitchen door at the side of the house, which is much handier for carrying things from the car. My sister rarely walks anywhere when she can drive. She claims she gets enough exercise working in her garden.

"Don't get out of the car," I said. "Sit tight while I call 999 on my mobile."

I made the call and we stayed put in the Mini with the doors locked to wait for the police to arrive. My normally bubbly sister had very little to say. Fortunately, we didn't have long to wait before a car carrying two police officers arrived. They instructed us to stay in the car while they checked to see if anyone was in the house. Hardly necessary of course, because we were far too frightened to get out. We watched the officers examine the front door first, then go down the path to the back of the house. They returned to the front and went in through the open door. After a short time, they came out to the Mini to tell us it was safe for us to go in to inspect the house for theft or damage.

The most obvious damage was to the front door jamb. It was badly splintered. The intruders must have used considerable force to burst the lock. The police officers accompanied us into the house. While they looked around, we went straight to Gabriella's little office to check on her desk computer. The lock on the office door had been forced, just like the one on the front door, and the wood around the lock splintered. On the desk where the computer had been, only the monitor, keypad, mouse and tangle of wires remained. Looking round the room it appeared that every drawer and cupboard in the office had been searched. Loose correspondence sat in little piles on the desk. Books from the bookshelf and the contents of her filing cabinet were neatly stacked on the table.

"They've certainly had a thorough rifle through," I said. "But look, Gabby, they haven't disarranged anything. It's all left neatly, ready for you to put back."

"I know. I suppose I should be glad of that but thank goodness I removed all my records. I'll soon sort the rest out."

We checked the rest of the house. Nothing had been damaged, but every room showed signs of a thorough search. In our bedrooms drawers and cupboards were open but everything was left in place. Likewise, the living room and the kitchen. As the police pointed out, with no car in the driveway it was a good guess that Gabriella might be out of the house for some time. There was no need for the intruders to rush the search. Nevertheless, breaking a door open, in broad daylight and in full view of the road, also suggested that the thieves were desperate to get in. The fact that they had searched in every room as well as taking the computer confirmed they were looking for something very specific and of great importance to them.

"Maybe something to do with your research, Dr Chester," one of the police officers suggested. "You know, your organic gardening is well known around here. My wife goes to your lectures."

Gabriella told them about the theft of her laptop from the kitchen table the previous day.

"I did report the laptop yesterday, so you should have a record of it. We weren't sure to begin with whether the thieves were just looking for small items they could sell. After this second time though, with my big computer gone, there's no question that they were looking for information about a research project I'm working on."

The officers assured her they would follow up on the case and advised her to call immediately if there should be any further developments.

It was late afternoon by the time the police left. I phoned Richard to tell him about the second break-in at Gabriella's. There was no reply, only the usual invitation to leave a message. Gabriella called her son George with the same result. Afterwards, she was very quiet. I put my arm around her.

"Gabs," I said, "unless you have anything else in the house your burglars might want, you've probably seen the last of them. In any case, there's nothing more we can do today and we haven't eaten since breakfast. How about I rustle up a light meal?"

That snapped my sister out of her melancholy. She jumped up.

"No thanks, Aggie, I'll do the lamb chops. We need comfort food after today and your cooking isn't great. Richard must be a saint to put up with it. You just sit down and recover."

I let the slur on my culinary competence pass, because my offer to cook had achieved its objective.

6

Richard did call back the following morning.

"Sorry I couldn't get back to you sooner. What's up?"

"I'm afraid there was another break in at Gabriella's yesterday. This time they've taken the desk computer from her office, the one she uses for her research. Her records are still safe, though, because she cleared them off the computer. They're all transferred to external drives and packed with other research files in her car boot."

"Another break-in? This is serious."

"I know."

"Her records may be safe for now, and you might even have another day before the thieves realise that they won't find what they want on the desk computer either. It's also possible they've discovered it already, so that's the assumption we've got to act on. Let me think for a moment. They obviously want that data very badly. They must somehow know that Gabriella refused a request to share it with someone at the Institute. Stealing it hasn't worked, because it wasn't on the computers. The only other way to get their hands on it is to approach Gabriella directly and persuade her to part with it — gently or otherwise."

"We hadn't thought of that. That's kind of scary, Richard."

"Yes, it is. Now, didn't you tell me she left her car at a garden centre?"

"Yes, but it's not in the general parking lot. It's hidden somewhere out of sight."

"That's fine, but these computer thefts were serious attempts to obtain Gabriella's composting records. If her work has potential financial implications, as she suggests it might, the situation could be dangerous. My guess, based on the lengths these people have gone to already, is that the next time they come to Bungay, it will be to corner Gabriella herself. If she isn't at home, they'll try to find her and one obvious place to look would be the local garden centre."

"Yes, you're right. It just hadn't occurred to us that they might come looking for Gabs."

"Well, think about it. And if they do enquire about her at the garden centre, it's quite likely that some helpful assistant would tell them she's gone away for a few days and that she left her car in the staff car park for safety while she's gone. Checking to see if her car was there would be a no-brainer."

"You're absolutely right," I said. "And if they spot her car and look in through the window, they could see the stuff she left on the back seat. It would be a no-brainer to look in the boot. Oh Richard, we have to get her car away from there. It's a pity that red Audi of hers is so conspicuous. Do you think we should risk going to retrieve it now, or would it be better to wait until it gets dark?"

"Neither. I think you should leave her car right where it is. Quick question though. Have you been parking your car on Gabriella's driveway or in the garage?"

"Oh, on the driveway all the time."

"Right, do you mind if I speak to Gabriella for a moment?"

I handed Gabriella my mobile, pressing the speaker button so I wouldn't miss anything.

"Tell me, Gabriella," I heard Richard say, "can you and Angelina drive her Mini to your car at the garden centre without any of their staff seeing you?"

"Oh yes, because the staff car park is behind the garden centre. You don't go into the garden centre to get there; you turn down a separate lane next to the main entrance. You don't see the lane from inside the centre."

"So, you and Angelina could drive to your car right now without anyone noticing you. Right?"

"Well yes, the lane doesn't lead to anywhere except the parking lot, and it's not staff leaving time or anything. The staff use a gate through into the garden centre and the gate has a number key lock so other people can't use it."

"Right, then I suggest the pair of you drive immediately to your car and transfer all your important stuff into the Mini. Then leave your car at the garden centre, locked just as before and set off for Scotland in Angelina's car."

"Scotland? At this time of day? Do you mean go all the way to Dunoon? We'll have to stop somewhere, Richard. We can't drive all through the night."

"Then get as far as you reasonably can before you stop for the night."

"Well okay, I suppose we can do that if you really think it's for the best."

"I do."

"Alright, we'll do as you say. We'll go to the garden centre to transfer my stuff to Aggie's car. Once we've done that, we can come back here to pack a few things and set off for Scotland."

"No, Gabriella! You're missing the point. You need to leave Bungay as soon as you've transferred your data to Angelina's car. Forget the packing. Whatever you do, don't go back to your house. It's just possible, those people may already be back looking for you. They may know you're using the Mini since it's been parked on your driveway. Go straight to the garden centre now, transfer your files to Angelina's car as quickly as you can, then hit the road. Try to avoid talking to anyone who sees you, but if they do, don't tell them where you're going."

Gabriella handed my mobile back to me.

"You heard all that, didn't you? Richard said they might be coming back for me. Oh Aggie, this is getting scary. Come on, we'd better hurry."

"Right Gabs, grab your handbag and look as though we're going shopping."

"What about your things?"

"Forget them. We mustn't draw attention to the fact that we're leaving. I've got my bag. That's all I need."

"Don't forget your jacket though."

"It's already in the boot."

We'd never know whether the house was under surveillance or not, or indeed if anyone noticed us leaving at all, but we went off in my car carrying only our handbags. Just in case anyone was interested where we were going, I drove straight to the shops, nipped in to a newsagent's and bought a newspaper. There were very few people on the street, and none appeared remotely interested us. There was no traffic on the road either. Reassured, I drove on to the garden centre.

Gabriella showed me where to turn into the lane which led to the employee car park. It was secluded and deserted. She had chosen a good hiding place for her car, over in the far corner and half hidden by shrubbery.

In her desperation, she had thrown piles of papers in rubber bands onto the back seat of her Audi, but the computer files she'd copied were locked safely in the boot, all in neat plastic folders. Retrieving them didn't take long and we got everything packed into the boot of the Mini easily. None of the garden centre staff came through the gate into the car park and no other vehicles had followed us down the lane. We gave each other the thumbs up, locked Gabriella's Audi, turned on its alarm, got into my car and drove off.

We had just turned into the lane which led out of the carpark, when another vehicle began to turn in from the road. To our horror it was a grey jeep. The lane was not wide enough for more than one car, so I had to reverse back into the car park to make way for it.

"Scrunch down in front of the seat," I said quickly to Gabriella, "keep your head down and pass me that woolly hat on the ledge in front of you."

Gabriella didn't need telling twice. She got right down with her head on the seat while I rammed the brown woolly hat over my hair and forehead and backed up to give the jeep access. Avoiding eye contact while cautiously observing the driver and passenger, I politely waved the jeep into the car park and exited without obvious haste down the lane.

Once on the road I turned towards the A143 out of Bungay. I was hoping we might have a few minutes' lead time while the thieves waited for the Audi alarm to stop and made sure no one came in response, before jimmying the boot open, only to find it empty. They might remember my car leaving the garden centre car park and come after us, of course, but at least we had a head start. I said so to Gabriella. She looked at me in amazement.

"I don't think so, Aggie," she said, "Those guys have no reason to be interested in my car. It's me they're after now, Richard said so. If they suspect it was me driving the Mini, they'll turn round right away and catch us up on the road. Look, I've got an idea. A friend of mine lives just round that bend ahead. Her drive winds round to the garage at the back of the house. We can hide in there. I'll tell you when to turn. It's on the left."

This was much more like my bossy sister, a sure sign that she was recovering, but what now?

7

There was no one home at Gabriella's friend's house, so instead of watching for the grey jeep in comfort, through the front window of the house, we were left with no choice but to watch from the garden, using a thick clump of bushes for cover. I left my red jacket in the car, which was safely parked behind the house, so that I would be less conspicuous, and the cold breeze blowing through the bushes really hit me as we crouched down among them.

"It's no use Gabs, I'm freezing," I whispered. "Either I put on my jacket and risk being seen, or you're going to have to watch by yourself."

"Is it lined?" she whispered back.

"Yes."

"Then turn it inside out so the red doesn't show."

I have to admit that Gabriella always could come up with practical solutions — not that I'd tell her so of course. I hurriedly retrieved my jacket from the car and put it on inside out so that it became an inelegant but nevertheless inconspicuous dull grey jacket instead of rather dashing bright red one. Gabriella smirked and nodded her approval when I re-joined her. She always did enjoy the opportunity to feel one up, being the younger twin by twenty minutes. Still, it was another sign she was recovering.

We didn't have to wait long. A grey jeep with a driver and a passenger passed the house along the A143, going west, the same route we were taking.

"Look," I breathed, "that's it Gabs. That's the jeep. I'm sure of it. Those are definitely the same two men that drove into the car park at the garden centre."

"I hope you're right," Gabriella said, "because I don't think we should stay here lurking in these bushes much longer. Someone might see us and call the police."

"Don't worry," I said confidently, "it was definitely them. Now that we've seen which way they went, we can just go the other way."

"I don't think going the other way will help us much if we want to get to Scotland as quickly as possible," she replied. "I just wonder if they're going to Cambridge. You know, Aggie, I'd hate to think this has anything to do with Cyril Jenkinson, you know, my colleague at the Agriculture Institute, the one who e-mailed me asking for information. It was an odd request really. He and I discussed my work, but it isn't really his field."

The implication of this information didn't hit me at the time. I was more concerned about our current predicament.

"Well never mind about that. Look, it's better that those guys in the jeep go on to Cambridge than stay around Bungay looking for you. As you say, we can't stay here in the bushes, but we can't take a chance driving on and risk being spotted either. The garden centre staff probably told them your car is a red

Audi, and they know that's still in the car park. When they saw the Mini leaving the car park, they probably thought I was you, so they'll almost certainly be looking for the Mini. What if they were to stop along the road for petrol and see us driving past?"

"I do hope they didn't break into my car."

"Don't worry, we took all your papers and files out."

"I'm thinking of the repair bill. I wish I hadn't locked it. I don't usually. I only locked it before because my data was in it."

"If they find you, you might have far more to worry about than a car repair bill. I'll tell you what, Gabs, I'll call Richard and see what he suggests we should do now. After all, he was the one who told us not to go back to your house and to get away from Bungay."

I called Richard but there was no reply. Instead, there was a message on my phone screen telling me he was unable to take my call but would call me back as soon as possible. How long would that be, I wondered. I showed the message to Gabriella.

"Well," she said, "in that case we'd better try George."

George is Gabriella's son. Until last year, we thought he was a civil servant working nine to five in a government office in London. He never corrected this assumption, somehow implying that his job was too boring to talk about. It turned out that he was actually a special intelligence agent for the government. We discovered this when he came up to Scotland to conduct an investigation and used my address without warning me that he was doing so. He imagined Aunt Aggie would never know and what she didn't know wouldn't hurt her. Silly man! George is my favourite nephew, but I wasn't too pleased with him that time.

As part of a ruse to flush out information leaks from a military base in Scotland, he mailed dummy reports to my address. This led to a bizarre series of attempts to retrieve the 'reports', during the course of which we discovered that not only was George a spook, but my retired neighbour and now husband, Richard Carter, had previously been one of his colleagues.

I handed Gabriella my phone. She gave George a quick rundown of our predicament.

"Richard knows all about it," I heard her say. "We've already tried to reach him. But we just got the automated reply saying he couldn't take the call. We just don't know how long it will be before he calls back, and George, we can't stay here. I've no idea when my friend will be back. If she comes soon we'll be alright, but for all I know she's away on holiday and might not be back for days, even weeks."

I watched Gabriella listening carefully to what George was saying.

"Well," she replied eventually, "if you're sure … all right, I'll tell Aggie."

Gabriella beckoned to me, "Come on. We don't need to stay out here in the bushes any longer. We're to wait in the car. If we're still here when my friend comes home, we just say we were passing, and I decided to drop by and introduce you before you go back to Scotland. I know it's not a very convincing explanation," she conceded, seeing me roll my eyes heavenwards, "but it's the only plausible one we have unless you can come up with a better one. And for heaven's sake Aggie, turn that jacket the right way out. It looks hideous."

"Fine," I said, nonchalantly taking off my inside-out jacket and right-siding it, "But what's the plan? What did George say? Are we just to sit in my car until Richard calls, or does he actually have a plan?"

Gabriella smirked. "We don't have to rely on Richard any longer. George is going to take care of things now."

That one-upmanship again! It's really not a pleasant trait in a sister.

"Gabriella," I said coldly (I don't often use her full name), "What exactly did George say? Exactly what are the things is he is going to take care of?"

Gabriella remained on her high horse. "He said we're to sit tight and he'll send help. He said they'll get here as soon as they can, but it might take up to an hour. It all depends on local availability."

"Availability of what?"

Gabriella didn't answer. She wasn't about to admit that she had no idea what George was planning for us. Ignoring me, she hurried to my car and got into the passenger seat. I shrugged and got into the car too. I handed her a chocolate bar from my emergency store in the glove compartment and the middle pages of the newspaper I bought on the way to the garden centre and settled down to read the outer pages myself while we waited. It was a local paper, and the news was mainly local things I knew nothing about, so it didn't take me long to reach the advertisement columns on the back pages. I was about to see if Gabriella was ready to swap her middle pages for the outside ones when a large notice in the middle of the last-but-one page caught my eye. I showed her the notice without bothering to read further myself.

"Here Gabs, look at this. Isn't this similar to the work you've been doing?"

COMPOST YOUR GARDEN WASTE
A lecture to be given by Professor Robert Smiley

She glanced casually at the notice at first, but then her eyes became riveted on it.

"I don't believe it!" she shrieked. "So that's why Cyril Jenkinson was after my results. They were going to present my work before I had time to publish it! I'm left out of the picture. Oh Aggie, I know exactly where he got the outline of my experiments from. He came to hear a lecture I gave to our local horticulture society last month. There was a lot of interest in the different approach I was taking and most of the horticulture department at the Agriculture Institute came over to hear it, including Cyril. I was still waiting for results at that time though. I'm scheduled now to give another lecture in a couple of months to present an interim report. I won't be ready until then."

I looked again at the notice and checked the date of the advertised lecture on my calendar.

"Gabs," I said, "this lecture is scheduled for the first Friday of next month and it's to be presented in a church hall in Cambridge. The notice says that a unique approach to composting will be presented by Professor R. G. Smiley. It doesn't say anything about a Cyril Jenkinson. Gabs, how serious are the commercial implications of all this?"

"Well," she said thoughtfully, "I'd say definitely not immediately. The results are very promising, quite exciting in fact, but a lot more work needs to be done to replicate and verify them before the technique would be commercially viable."

"The technique? Seriously Gabs, you're talking about an actual technique for composting garden muck. Isn't a good rake over enough?"

"Oh, quite a bit more than a muck rake, I can assure you."

I thought for a moment to digest this mind-blowing information.

"Gabs," I said, "I think you may be too close to all this to see clearly what's going on. I'm looking in from the outside so maybe it's easier for me to see the big picture."

"What big picture?"

"It's about money and prestige! Think about it. A female amateur gardener, albeit with a fair amount of research experience during her working years, comes up with a new and effective composting technique that the horticulture professionals had never even thought about. Think of the blow to their pride! What conceivable right have you encroach on their territory? The whole world knows they are the experts on anything to do with horticulture. It can't be countenanced!"

"But they're not like that in the horticulture department, Aggie." she said, "They've always been very welcoming and willing to discuss anything with me. In fact, right up to now, Cyril and I have been the best of friends. I just can't believe he would do a thing like this without telling me."

I did notice that her face had gone a little pink but at the time put it down to the heat of the moment.

"The thing is, Gabs," I said, "while they saw you as simply an enthusiastic gardener, you were no threat to them. But now, all on your own you've developed this new, unique composting technique, and you've been giving public lectures about it. You say the process needs further research. That means you may eventually need outside funding, which is the life-blood of academic research. Think about it, Gabby, your work has surpassed any composting research they're doing so there's a possibility you could be in competition with them for funding, particularly if your technique could be developed commercially. You've invaded their territory."

"Oh dear, I certainly didn't mean to."

"And think about the possible commercial implications," I continued. "If it proves to be successful, some commercial outfit might want to buy exclusive rights to the technique. I'm not sure, but I think that involves owning the patent."

Gabriella sighed. "Oh Aggs, all I've been looking for is a simple, organic way to help gardeners to get the best from their flowers and veg."

"Unfortunately, not everyone's that altruistic, Gabby. You know, I just can't imagine where all this is going to lead."

8

We didn't have long to wait before a tow truck backed up the driveway to the back of Gabriella's friend's house. I watched in the car mirror as the driver jumped out of his cab and walked over to the Mini. I lowered my window cautiously. He leaned down and stared at the two of us intently then signalled us to come out.

"I'm to tow your car away," he informed us. "No mistaking you're the right ones. Like as two peas you are!"

I backed my car carefully up to the truck and watched anxiously as the driver attached the towing equipment. I hoped he knew what he was doing. My Mini was only a year old.

"Right," he said, climbing back into his cab, "I'll be off."

"Just a minute," Gabriella shrieked, "what about us?"

The driver looked perplexed.

"Sorry ladies, my instructions are to collect the car. I wasn't told anything about you."

"But surely," I said, "we can ride in the cab with you. We don't mind squeezing up together."

"No," Gabriella affirmed, "we don't mind squeezing up at all."

"It's not that I wouldn't take you, ladies," he replied, "even though they didn't tell me to. It's just that there's no room for you. Have a look for yourselves."

He waved a hand towards the cab. "There's hardly enough room up there for me and Jasper."

I looked. Peering down from the cab and regarding the scene with great interest, and taking up most of the bench seat, was an enormous Great Dane.

"Now just you stay there, Jasper," the driver admonished him. "I'm coming up."

There was nothing we could do but look on anxiously as my Mini was towed away. We no longer had a car to sit and wait in.

"Oh Aggie," Gabriella wailed, "I've just remembered, our handbags are still in the car."

"Never mind." I spoke more cheerfully than I felt. "All is not lost. We still have our mobiles so you can call George again. He must have forgotten that we need to be rescued as well as the car. Men can be very single-minded you know. All you have to do is remind him gently that we're stranded here."

That got Gabriella refocussed as I expected it would. She can't bear to hear anyone criticise her son, even mildly. She's the only person allowed to do that.

"Of course he didn't forget us!" she snapped. "I don't know why you don't have more confidence in George. Obviously, he has a plan for us as well as the car. Just be patient. You'll see."

Gabriella stomped back behind the house. That killed my solution to our problem temporarily. She could be stubborn, but I knew she would calm down and call George eventually. As it happened, we didn't have to wait for her to settle down because almost as soon as the tow truck left, a grey Honda saloon turned into the driveway. Naturally we assumed it would be Gabriella's friend returning home. I followed her as she rushed up to the car. We had discussed this eventuality. She had decided to explain that my car had broken down right outside the house and had to be towed away. She would say that we were waiting in the driveway so as to be off the road and were just about to call a taxi to take us home. To our surprise, this flaky explanation was not needed. It was not her friend driving the Honda after all. It was a young man wearing a red baseball cap. We backed away hastily, but the driver lowered his window and beckoned.

"I'm here to collect you," he called. "Hop in."

We rushed joyfully to the Honda.

"Thank goodness there wasn't room for us in the tow truck cab!" I said as we clambered into the back seat of the Honda. "This will be a much more comfortable ride."

We only thought to question the driver after the car moved off.

"Thank you for coming for us," I said, hoping my voice didn't reveal my near panic. "But we'd like to know who sent you to collect us and where you're planning to take us."

Gabriella looked at me in consternation, the implications of getting into the car without question now dawning on her too.

"Mr Chester's instructions," he replied cheerfully as he started his engine, "and I'm to drive you to Cambridge."

Gabriella and I looked at each other in relief at the mention of George.

"I'm to take you to a hotel. Mr Chester said I was to tell you to wait for him in the hotel restaurant. He'll get there as soon as he can."

"Oh! Well, did Mr Chester say when he expects to get there?" asked Gabriella.

"He didn't say. He only said to tell you to you wait for him in the restaurant."

"Did he say anything about my car?" I asked. "Only, it's a new car and I wouldn't want it to get damaged by being towed."

"I wouldn't worry ma'am," the driver said cheerfully. "It wouldn't have needed to be towed away if there wasn't something wrong with it already. The repair shop will sort it out, make it as good as new."

Gabriella's warning look prevented me just in time from exclaiming indignantly that there was nothing wrong with my car. Chastened, I sat back and let her take over the questions.

"Did Mr Chester happen to mention if the car was being taken to Cambridge too?" she asked casually. "I do hope so, because all our clothes and things are in it. We'll need to get them."

The 'things' Gabriella was concerned about of course were her research notes and files in the boot.

"All our luggage is still in the boot of my sister's

car," she said. "That's why we need to find out where it's being towed to."

I nodded in agreement. I was concerned about our handbags as well as the contents of Gabriella's plastic folders.

"Oh yes, we'll certainly need our things out of the car."

"I'd guess they would tow your car to Cambridge too," the driver speculated. "It would make sense, since that's where Mr Chester's going to meet you, but I'm only guessing. I don't know for certain. You'll have to ask the boss. Why don't you call him now?"

Gabriella took her mobile out of her pocket, but I quickly put my hand over it. There was no reason to suspect the driver, but I had learned from Richard that one should never give away information to strangers. If my car had been taken to Cambridge, we could easily retrieve it.

"There's no need to bother about my car just now, Gabs," I said hurriedly. "It can wait until we meet up with George. If the car is in Cambridge, he'll take us along to get our things."

"I can put the car on speakerphone if you want to call," the driver said helpfully, his hand moving towards a switch.

But Gabriella had picked up on my hesitation.

"Thank you, but no, it won't be necessary," she said. "I'm sure Mr. Chester will sort it out when he arrives."

9

The hotel we were taken to was on the outskirts of Cambridge. I was surprised to see so many cars in the parking bay that ran the length of the front of the hotel. There was also a large sign indicating additional parking available to the rear. The answer became clear as soon as we went in. This was a popular venue for business meetings. The tables in the restaurant leading off the lobby were occupied by smartly dressed men and women. Many of the chairs were turned towards a speaker on a raised platform at the far end of the room. All attention was focussed on the speaker, so Gabriella and I were able to slip unnoticed into seats at an empty table at the back of the room, where I learned rather more than I wished to know about marketing bathroom porcelain. Gabriella was fascinated though.

George arrived as the business meeting was winding up, impatient to find out what was going on.

"Right, Mum," he greeted his mother, "Dick called me and said he told you to go to the garden centre in Bungay to transfer some files to Aunt Aggie's car and that you were planning to drive up to Scotland with them. He knew he would be tied up for the next few hours so asked me to keep an eye on the pair of you. Then I got an urgent call from you saying you were hiding at the back of someone's house in Bungay and needed to be rescued. What kind of pickle have you got yourself into this time?"

Pickle indeed! This was not a game. The sooner George understood the seriousness of the situation the better. Since we'd had nothing to eat since breakfast, I suggested we adjourn to the hotel coffee shop to eat while we talked. Over tea and sandwiches, Gabriella, the drama queen, gave him a colourful, albeit accurate rundown on the day's events.

I pointed out that I had not spoken to Richard since we set off for the garden centre and that we should let him know that we were now in Cambridge instead of *en route* to Scotland.

"Actually," George smirked, "I've already told him." I turned away so that he would not see me roll my eyes heavenwards. Not however before I noticed Gabriella also smirking fondly with him. Those two are so alike!

"George," I said firmly, "we won't be going anywhere until we get my car back. Our handbags are in it as well as your mother's research records. If you wouldn't mind taking us to it, we'll be out of your hair."

George grinned. "Come on then." He led the way to the car park extension at the back of the hotel. His was the only car parked there, so the bathroom porcelain meeting must have finished. I noticed he was using a rental car. He didn't speak as he drove us to an industrial estate a few miles away. To my surprise, he used an automatic garage door opener at the entrance to a large building. We drove in. He immediately clicked the door shut behind us, then drove the car into a parking bay at one side of the building.

"Before you ask," George said quietly as we got out of the car, "the answer is 'No', I'm not going to explain anything. Just be glad that I happened to be in the vicinity when you called, okay?"

Gabriella and I both nodded. We had previous experience of George's access to such resources last year when he involved me in that cloak and dagger chase around the country over some missing correspondence. We might learn more later, but now was not the time. I looked round the enormous building. It was well lit. At one side there were rooms with closed doors. At the far end there were open shelves and cubbies filled with what looked like electronic gadgetry and mechanical equipment. Cars, including the one we arrived in, were parked along the other side of the building.

Gabriella was peering intently at the row of parked cars. She nudged me and hissed in my ear, "Look Aggie, have you noticed something rather peculiar?"

I hadn't but wasn't about to admit it.

"Yes," I whispered mendaciously, "I wonder if you noticed the same thing as me?"

"Mother," George looked cross, "I've got to get the two of you on your way as quickly as possible, so stop whispering and pay attention. What are you whispering about anyway?"

Gabriella beamed self-importantly.

"It's just that I noticed, and so did Aggie," she looked at me for confirmation, "that those cars along the wall are all from different rental companies."

"Yes," I chimed in, now realising what I was supposed to have noticed, "and the car you brought us here in is from a rental company too."

Gabriella looked at the car quickly to confirm this.

"Yes," she said, "I noticed that too." She hadn't of course.

"Right," said George, neatly shutting off further discussion of rental cars, "the first thing we have to do is to get you fixed up with wheels."

"Oh good!" I exclaimed, spotting my blue Mini three cars along the row, dwarfed and almost hidden by a people carrier. I rushed joyfully towards it. "Here we are, Gabs, here's my Mini. Now we can be on our way."

"You can certainly be on your way, Aunt Aggie," George called after us, "but not in your Mini. That's potentially a marked car now."

I must have looked crestfallen at this because he continued gently, "Don't worry, I've got another car waiting for you and Mother to drive to Scotland. How about one of these?"

He waved towards the row of cars parked along the wall.

"I thought you might like this BMW3 series. Honestly, Aunt Ag, don't worry, we'll ship your car up to Scotland once you get home."

"I'll answer for both of us," exclaimed Gabriella, delighted with the prospect of driving the BMW.

"George, you're a genius! The BMW will be perfect. Come on Aggie, let's transfer all the stuff out of your Mini."

I didn't care for the implication that the BMW would be preferable to my Mini to drive to Scotland, but recognised the necessity to change cars, so let it pass. George was doing his best for us.

"Do we have to return the car to its rental company when we get home?" I asked. "Only I'm not at all sure we have that company anywhere near where I live. I've never even heard of Beechcroft Motors before."

George pulled a mobile out of his pocket and touched it — presumably a name on his contact list — because he then spoke briefly into the phone. One of the doors on the other side of the building opened and out stepped the driver of the grey Honda who brought us to Cambridge. George pointed to the BMW.

"That one please, Bob," he said, pointing to the BMW. The driver went over to the BMW and peeled off the rental car markings. He spent a few minutes checking it over.

"We'll pick up the BMW when we deliver your Mini, Aunt Ag," George told me. "You'd better be setting off now. Bob tells me the tank is full. Would you like me to arrange a hotel for you tonight, say at Grantham?"

"I think we might get as far as York if I'm driving," Gabriella said airily, "but don't bother to find us a hotel, love, leave it to us. That way we can stop wherever we like. Just tell us how to get to the A1 from here."

"You've got a Sat-Nav in the car, Mother. I'll just set it for York. You know your way well enough once you get there."

That was true. Gabriella and I grew up in York.

It didn't take us many minutes to transfer her files from my car boot to that of the BMW, collect our purses and hit the road. Gabriella was happy to be at the wheel and I was even happier to let her. After all, I had driven south to Bungay almost non-stop a couple of days ago. I fell asleep almost as soon as we left Cambridge and woke only to hear Gabriella declare jubilantly, "We're here! Time to wake up."

The daylight was already fading. We were in fact in a car park. Gabriella must have driven all the way from Cambridge to York while I slept. The car park belonged to a hotel beside the River Ouse that both Gabriella and I knew very well. It was a frequent overnight stop-off point for both of us on our visits to each other.

"Come on, let's see if they have a room for us." Gabriella was already out of the car. "I'll just double check that the boot's locked." She checked and nodded. "All OK."

The car park was full of cars and Gabriella had done well to find a space because many of the cars would belong to diners rather than residents. The hotel restaurant is well known in York for its excellent cuisine and is invariably busy in the evenings.

We did manage to get a room for the night, but neither of us felt up to facing the bustle of the restaurant and possibly having to wait for a table, so we treated ourselves to a room service dinner. Despite having slept on the journey I fell asleep as soon as my head touched the pillow. Gabriella, who had far more reason to be exhausted than I had, did likewise.

10

Gabriella and I left our hotel in York after an early breakfast on Thursday morning, and set off for Scotland before the roads got busy. Gabriella insisted on driving and I was happy to let her. We made good time going north and crossed the Firth of Clyde on the car ferry from McInroy's Point, Gourock, to Hunters Quay, Dunoon, arriving home in time for a late lunch. We had to make do with tinned soup and peanut butter on oatcakes. More esoteric fare was not on offer until I went shopping because I'd thrown all perishable food away before setting off for Bungay on Monday, expecting to be gone for a couple of weeks.

Before shopping though, I decided to go through the mail that had accumulated in my absence. Leaflets and letters lay on the floor under the letterbox, which I collected and took into the living room. Gabriella was already stretched out in a recliner chair with the footrest horizontal, enjoying a well-earned rest after her long drive. I rifled through the wad of mail in my hand. There appeared to be nothing that required immediate attention, so I took it along to my office to sort out and to check the accumulated email as well. Like Gabriella, I use one of the bedrooms as an office.

"I'm afraid you're in the smallest bedroom this time," I informed her. "We needed the larger one to accommodate Richard's desk as well as mine when we opted to live in this house rather than in his. Hope you don't mind."

"Fine," said Gabriella without opening her eyes. "Makes no difference to me so long as you didn't put a smaller bed in it."

'No," I smiled, "it's the same bed. Anyway, I'm going to go through my mail now. I shouldn't be long so you can use the computer if you need it after you've had a nap."

"Thanks, Aggie, I'll do that later if you don't mind. Just now I'm just going to relax and rest my eyes for a while."

She was already half asleep. I tiptoed out of the room, closing the door so as not to disturb her, and went to my desk.

The mail I had picked up from the hall floor was quickly dealt with and mostly consigned to the recycle bin. Most of the emails awaiting my attention were simply junk too and were likewise binned.

One email did catch my attention though. It was from a Cyril Jenkinson. I recalled hearing that name recently from Gabriella. It was back at Bungay when we were hiding in the Mini behind her friend's house, reading the local newspaper. I'd shown her a notice announcing a lecture on new developments on composting. The lecture was to be given in Cambridge by a professor from the Agriculture Institute. That was when the name came up. Cyril Jenkinson was

Gabriella's contact at the Institute, the one who emailed her requesting her compost research data. She'd emailed back, saying that more work needed to be done before the data would be ready to be shared. I remembered her worried look when she told me that for some reason she had felt uneasy about that email and that she had always liked Cyril Jenkinson.

I clicked on the email:

Dear Ms Maud,

I am a friend and colleague of Dr Gabriella Chester. I have been trying to contact her for the past two days but she has not returned my emails or phone calls so I am presuming she must be away. She has mentioned your name once or twice in conversation. In fact, she was telling me only recently that you are planning to visit her. Do you know how or where I might contact her? I would greatly appreciate your help.

Sincerely,
Cyril Jenkinson

I read the email a second time. Alarm bells rang in my head. Cyril Jenkinson could only have got my email address and discovered that I was planning to visit Gabriella by reading my Monday morning email to her, and that email was on her laptop computer. He must be the one behind the two break-ins in Bungay. He claimed to have a chatty relationship with Gabriella but breaking into her house and stealing her computers was hardly the action of a friend. Then again, if she considered Cyril Jenkinson a close enough friend to discuss her family with him, she would surely have identified me as her sister even if she had not mentioned the 'Dr'. No, this Cyril Jenkinson was obviously fishing for information on Gabriella's whereabouts. He sent that email hoping she had been in touch with me, and that I would tell him where to find her.

That was one email I was not going to respond to.

I went back into the living room to show Gabriella the email and get her reaction, only to find her now fast asleep in the chair. It would be unkind to wake her after that long drive, so I spread a rug over her and went back to my office to call Richard and discuss the matter with him. Once again however, I got a recorded message saying that he would call back as soon as he could. I might have called George at that point if I had known his number. Gabriella had it but I didn't. Since I could do nothing more about the email until either she woke or Richard called back, I went to the kitchen and made a cup of tea. After all, we were a long way from Bungay and Cambridge. Gabriella's data was locked safely in the boot of the BMW, and the BMW was safely locked in my garage here in Dunoon. There was really no need to worry about Cyril Jenkinson's email. Or was there? I was about to find out.

11

The telephone rang. It was the land line, which now-adays serves primarily for broadband access since we have all started using mobiles. I expected it would be a cold call. From time to time, I arrange to stop them but somehow they always manage to start again. Should I bother to answer it? Well, I had nothing else to do while waiting for my husband to call and for my sister to wake up. I picked up the kitchen extension.

A female voice asked, "Is that Ms Maud?

I waited for the caller to elaborate. This gives the legitimate caller time to identify themselves before I put the receiver down on a cold call.

"Ms Maud?"

I continued to wait.

"Am I speaking to Ms Maud?"

Still, I waited. I heard background discussion. I could just make out a male voice saying, "Thank you, I'll take it from here, close the door as you leave."

A pompous male voice now came onto the line. "Ms Maud, I sent you an email."

I was not about to reply.

"Ms Maud, maybe my secretary didn't tell you who was calling. This is Professor Cyril Jenkinson speaking from the Agriculture Institute, Cambridge."

I had already suspected as much, of course.

"Speaking," I replied at last. Did I hear a sigh of relief at the other end of the line? His words followed in a rush.

"Ms Maud, you may have heard of me from your friend Dr Gabriella Chester. I sent you an email but I'm guessing you may not have read it yet. Briefly, I'm trying to locate Dr Chester and have been unable to contact her at her home. She recently mentioned you were going to visit her in Bungay, so I'm contacting you because I thought maybe you would have some idea of her whereabouts."

"Excuse me," I said hastily, "I can hear the doorbell. I'm sorry but I have to go. Let me call you back later. Bye!"

I put down the receiver quickly. Now what? I went back to my computer and pulled up Cyril Jenkinson's email again on my laptop and reread it.

'*Dear Ms Maud*,' it began.

I didn't change my email address when I married Richard, so 'Ms Maud' was a probably a reasonable guess at my identity. Cyril Jenkinson would have found my telephone number alongside my email address on the contact list that I know Gabriella keeps on her laptop.

It went without saying that I was not going to respond to either the email or the telephone call. So long as no one knew Gabriella was in Scotland she should be safe here. Cyril Jenkinson was obviously hoping she had been in contact with me since she left Bungay and that she had told me where she was going. I had no intention of helping him. That was the end of that.

I was still in my office, catching up on other correspondence when the landline rang again. This time I ignored it. When the ringing stopped, the message box clicked in and I listened to the recording:

"Ms Maud, this is Professor Jenkinson again. Please call me back at this number."

I took a pencil and notepad and, although I had no intention of calling him back, wrote the number down. It was a different number from the one logged on my phone readout panel for his previous call. In fact, it looked like a mobile number. That reminded me to put my own mobile on charge. I had not done so since leaving here on Monday to visit Gabriella.

My sister was stirring when I went back into the living room.

"Did I hear the phone ring just then?" she asked, still half asleep. "I didn't hear you answer it."

"Yes, you heard it ring," I confirmed. "And no, I didn't answer it and if it rings again Gabs, don't you answer it either."

"Why ever not? Who was calling?"

I smiled grimly, "Cyril Jenkinson."

"Cyril! Oh Aggie!" she gasped; her face quite flushed. "I must definitely talk to Cyril if he calls again. I'm quite sure he had nothing to do with those two men that broke into my house and stole my computers. Cyril would never do such a thing. Seriously Aggie he's well he's just … not that sort of person."

This was a most unexpected reaction. She must be still half asleep. I hastened to put her right. "Gabby, you told me that the first time those men broke into your house and stole your laptop was after you responded to an email from Cyril Jenkinson requesting access to your research data. You said that you replied straight away and explained that it wasn't quite ready to share. I know you said earlier you didn't think he could be involved, but just come into my office and look at an email I received from him."

Gabriella followed me into my office and read the email.

"He says nothing about my research in this email, Aggie," she pointed out, somewhat defensively, I thought. "Nothing at all. All he says is that he wants to get in touch with me."

I reread the email. It was true, there was no reference to Gabriella's research.

"Well," I said, "why would he say anything about your research to me? He obviously thinks I'm just a friend who was planning to visit you in Bungay, nothing to do with your research. There's no reason for him to think I know anything about the theft of your computers."

"Well, he says he's been trying to reach me. Aggie, he had nothing to do with the computer thefts, he just wants to get in touch with me."

Now my sister has always been very astute, uncomfortably so at times. I couldn't understand why she was so determined to give this man the benefit of the doubt. Why, in the face of irrefutable evidence, was she telling me she doubted Cyril Jenkinson's involvement? He may have been a good friend to her in the past, but his present actions were far from those of a friend. To me they suggested serious and possibly dangerous professional rivalry.

"Look Gabby," I said firmly, "Cyril Jenkinson could only have known I was planning to visit you from that email I sent you just before your laptop was stolen. That can only mean he has access to your emails, which in turn implies he has at least one of your computers, if not both. Where else could he have got my email address, even if you did mention my name to him at some time or other?"

"I just don't understand it." Gabriella looked perplexed. "I know Cyril would never..."

I'd had enough.

"Well," I snapped, "just listen to this!"

With a flourish I pressed the 'play' button on the telephone console.

Gabriella listened to the recording then replayed it. She replayed it a second time, listening intently, then turned to me.

"That's not Cyril! Aggie, that's definitely not Cyril's voice!"

I couldn't believe it. Why was she still defending the man?

"Gabby," I said, "I know he's your friend and I can see that you're having difficulty thinking he might be after your research material, but surely..."

"No Aggie," she insisted, "listen again. Please."

Together we listened again to the recording.

"That's not Cyril's voice!"

I looked at her for an explanation.

"That's not Cyril's voice," she insisted again. "Listen carefully. Can you hear it? That's Thames Estuary speak. Cyril doesn't talk like that, he's a Yorkshireman. He has a northern accent."

I took a deep breath, "OK Gabs," I said carefully, "but I have to tell you, there was an earlier call while you were asleep. The caller identified himself as Professor Cyril Jenkinson. It was the same voice as the one you've just heard. He called because I had not responded to the email he sent — which, as you can see, is signed Cyril Jenkinson."

"Goodness Aggie, what did you say to him?"

"Oh, nothing really. I just said I had to go and answer the doorbell and that I'd call him back."

"Oh Aggie, you didn't call him back, did you? Please say you didn't."

"No, of course I didn't. That's why he called again and left that message."

"Well, it certainly wasn't Cyril."

"Look Gabby," I said, "if the voice on the box isn't your friend Cyril's, then someone else is impersonating him to get to you. It has to be someone who knows of your friendship and for some reason thinks I know of it too. He was banking on Cyril's name being enough to allay any reservations I might have about discussing you with him. He's also someone who knows enough about your research to want to steal it. Now, can you think of anyone who might want to get their hands on your data? What about the voice — does that help identify him?"

She shook her head. "I can't think of any of our colleagues, either at the Institute or anywhere else, that would get involved in this. And as for the voice, that slightly Southern accent, that could be any of at least a dozen guys I know in the Horticulture Department."

"Well," another thought came to me, "I could tell that the first phone call came from an office, and the second was from a mobile number. Look, the number is on the log. Do you recognise it?"

Gabriella looked at the number logged and the one I had written down.

"Why, yes," she said. "The number logged has the same prefix as one I use to contact the horticulture department. Aggie, I think I can clear the mystery up very quickly. I've got Cyril's mobile number, so I'll call him now and ask him if he's been looking for me."

That seemed to make sense, but I had a sudden thought.

"Hold on, Gabby," I said, "just check the work number you have for Cyril against this number. I thrust my telephone notepad in front of her. She looked at the number and gasped.

"I don't believe it! That *is* Cyril's number, look." She pulled her mobile out of her pocket, scrolled down the contact list and clicked on his name.

"Oh, Aggie," she wailed. "It can't be."

I compared the two numbers. "Gabs, look more carefully. These two numbers look the same at first glance, but the final digit is different."

Gabriella looked at the numbers and breathed a sigh of relief. "Thank heavens it's not his number!"

Were those tears in her eyes? I couldn't be sure because she turned away quickly. At any rate, she recovered quickly, saying, "It has to be an Agriculture Institute number though, and close enough to belong to the same department as Cyril."

12

"What do you fancy for dinner today, Gabs?' I asked. "You have a choice. We can go shopping for something or we can eat out."

"You mean you haven't even got eggs and a bit of bacon in the house?"

"I think there might be one egg in the fridge, but no bacon. There'll be a tin of beans in the cupboard too, but I gave my bread to the birds before setting off for Bungay."

"Have you got hot chocolate?"

'Yes, but no milk."

Gabriella rolled her eyes, "Pass me a pen and paper and I'll make a list. You never were much good at planning ahead, Aggie."

Gabriella had always been free with criticism, but I'd managed to distract her from that pesky Cyril Jenkinson she insisted on defending.

My local supermarket is a couple of miles along the coast road so we set off in the BMW, Gabriella at the wheel. I still hadn't got to drive it, even though I am the older twin by twenty minutes. She can be selfish too.

"Are you in a snit about something, Aggs?" Gabriella grinned You're muttering to yourself."

"Rubbish!" I retorted. "I was just clearing my throat."

"Something about twenty minutes."

"I may have said something about plenty of biscuits. I don't think you put biscuits on the shopping list."

She snorted and did a showy turn into one of the parking slots at the supermarket and ended up too close to the next car to open her door to get out. I politely refrained from comment as she reversed the BMW, centred it, then parked neatly as she should have done the first time. I noticed that the driver of a grey VW Golf that followed us into the car park seemed to be taking a great interest as he waited for these manoeuvres to finish so he could park his own car further along the line. Serves her right, I thought, still not at all pleased with her.

"Why don't you go on ahead and start shopping," I suggested as we got out of the car. "I'm just going to nip along to the chemist along the road. I'll catch you up inside the store."

As I strode off to cross the road I heard a male voice behind me. The accent was Thames Estuary.

"Excuse me."

There was no reason to suppose he was speaking to me so I paid no attention. Not, that is, until I heard his next words.

"Dr Gabriella Chester, I thought I recognised you driving the BMW. I'm so glad to see you."

I felt rigid with shock. Forcing myself to appear calm, I turned round to see the driver of the Golf who had been watching Gabriella's manoeuvrings in the car park. I had a sudden awful thought that this might be the fake Cyril Jenkinson. Surely not. It couldn't be.

"I'm afraid I don't recall…" I said, playing for time.

"No, no, of course you wouldn't. You don't know me at all, but I remember you very well. My wife and I once heard you give a lecture on care of roses to a horticulture group in Norwich. It was a couple of years ago, but I still remember it well. We were visiting my in-laws. They were keen to hear your talk and we went along with them.

"Actually," I said, having managed to collect my wits somewhat while he was speaking, "I'm not Dr Chester. Perhaps I look a little like her."

Miracles do happen. At that critical moment when I had no idea what to say or do next, one of my neighbours drove into the car park. She stopped beside us and lowered her window.

"Angelina!" she called, "I'm so glad I caught you — saves me a phone call and I could only call when Andrew is out. I want to give him a surprise birthday party two weeks on Saturday. I'm inviting some of the neighbours. Do you think you and your husband will be able to come? Please say yes."

"Offhand I'd say yes, but I'll check my calendar and confirm," I replied. "I know we'd love to."

Surely, after overhearing this neighbourly exchange, the man who thought I was Gabriella would take the hint and drift away. He didn't though; but stayed doggedly beside me. I had to convince him somehow that I was not Gabriella, so I gestured to him and continued:

"You'll never guess what, Jean, this gentleman has just mistaken me for an expert on rose growing."

"That's a good one," Jean laughed. "Angelina has many talents," she told the stranger, "but I wouldn't say that gardening is one of them. Sorry hen," she turned back to me, "but you've got to admit a bit of weeding wouldn't come amiss in your garden."

Another car honked behind her; she was blocking the way. She waved to me and to the car and moved along.

"I'm so sorry," said the man awkwardly. "It was two years ago, but it was a great lecture and you reminded me so much of Dr Chester."

"I'm flattered if anything," I replied, then had a sudden thought. I asked him, "Are you on holiday here?"

"As a matter of fact, we are. My wife and I rented a holiday lodge here in Dunoon for a week. Unfortunately, we have to leave on Saturday. We're hoping this splendid weather continues because we're doing a short Highland tour before that long drive home."

"How far do you have to go?" I asked as casually as I could, although I was aching to know the answer.

"York," he said.

I almost sighed with relief, until he added, "We'll stay in York a couple of days to break the journey and visit friends there. Then on home to Cambridge."

Cambridge. I nearly died.

Forcing myself to look cheerful, I bade the man goodbye, nice to have met you etc., and set off for the chemist. Halfway across the road I suddenly realised that he might see Gabriella when he went inside the store. He would know immediately it wasn't me again because Gabriella was wearing a blue jacket and I my faithful red one.

I did some quick thinking. It was most likely that this man had nothing to do with the attempts to steal Gabriella's research data. He could, however, on his return to Cambridge, innocently mention to the wrong people that while on holiday in Dunoon he had met the great Dr Chester in a supermarket. If that happened, Gabriella would no longer be safe here.

It was just possible, too, that he was in fact the Cyril Jenkinson impersonator, who just happened to be on holiday here in Dunoon. He could easily have arranged the computer thefts with accomplices back in Cambridge and he could just as easily have instigated a search for Gabriella from Dunoon as from Cambridge. In that case, she could be in immediate danger of discovery. I had to warn her. I pulled out my mobile.

"Gabs," I whispered into the phone although there was no one close enough to hear me, "Where in the store are you?"

"You've been so long that I've already done the shopping. I'm just about to be checked out."

"Right," I said. "Listen, you'll never guess what's happened. I've just been mistaken for Dr Gabriella Chester by a man from Cambridge. Right now, he's in the car park. I can see that he's picked up a trolley from the stack and he's wheeling it towards the

store. Gabs, you've got to get out of the store before
he sees you. I'll explain later, but right now, keep
your face turned towards the window, away from
the aisles. When you're checked out, don't go to the
door that goes out to the car park. Instead, take the
first exit you come to. It's on your right and goes out
to the road. I'll meet you just outside."

Gabriella has always been quick on the uptake; I'll
give her that. She hustled out of the door in less than
two minutes carrying her bulging shopping bags.

"What's this all about, Aggie?"

"Quickly!" I almost pushed her and the two shopping bags into a lane beside the store that leads into
a small park. "We need a quick exit, Gabs," I told her.
"Walk straight along that path through the park
until you get to the road. Turn right, then cross the
road and keep walking. You'll be on the left-hand
side. I'll go and get the car and come and pick you up
along the road."

She nodded. "Okay, but can you take these bags
with you to the car please, they're quite heavy."

"Sorry, I can't," I replied. "That guy took a lot of
convincing. He saw me going across the road. I can't
suddenly appear in the car park with a large bag of
groceries. Just give me the car keys and I'll be as quick
as I can."

I hurried back to the car park, got into the BMW
and began to drive out. To my consternation, I noticed a grey car in the driving mirror, which was
also heading for the exit. There were no other cars
between us and it was gaining on me. Realistically,

I knew it could not possibly be the man from Cambridge because he could not have done his shopping and got back to his car in that short time. Just to be sure though, instead of turning right to pick up Gabriella I turned left and left again onto the coast road. The grey car was still behind me, but I wasn't able to see who was driving it. I took a left turn off the coast road and it didn't follow. It was almost certainly not the Cambridge man's car, and if it had been it probably wouldn't have mattered whether he saw me or not. Nevertheless, I felt better, virtuous in fact, for having taken evasive action. I made my way back to collect Gabriella, expecting commendation. Instead, I got a very indignant reception.

"Where on earth have you been all this time? You've had time to collect the car twice over. Look how far I've had to walk, carrying these two heavy bags."

13

Richard called that evening and I brought him up to date with all that had happened since he urged us to leave Bungay. Was that really only yesterday?

"You and Gabriella did very well getting away from Bungay the way you did," he said. "You showed great enterprise."

Now, I thought that statement was rather patronising, but I let it go. This was no time to quibble. We both knew very well Richard had asked George to arrange our rescue from Bungay. George arranged for my tell-tale Mini to be spirited away, sent a car to take us from Bungay to Cambridge, met us in Cambridge and then lent us the BMW for the rest of our journey north. I simply said, "Gabriella and I couldn't have done it without help from you and George. We're very grateful to you both."

"Well," he said, "I was certainly relieved when George called to let me know you got away from Cambridge without any problem. And it's good to know that you're safely home at last. All we have to do now is track down the villain who is after your sister's research. That shouldn't be difficult. You know, only your sister could get herself into such a to-do over a pile of garden muck. I'm so glad I chose the right sister!"

"I'm glad too," I sighed, remembering there was a time when Gabriella had set her sights on Richard. I was never sure at the time whether Richard was aware of this or not. I certainly hadn't been about to put the idea into his head. Now I realised he had known all along, he just never let on. Hmm! Time to change the subject.

"By the way, how much longer do you think you'll be away on your assignment?"

"It isn't going to take as long as I thought, so I should be home by the middle of next week. In fact, I may drive your Mini up myself if it hasn't been returned to you by then."

"That'll be great."

"In the meantime, though, you'll have to be particularly careful. Whatever you do, don't take the BMW out again, either you or Gabriella. I agree with you that it's unlikely that the man you met today has any connection to the people who are after her research, but on the off chance that there is a link, that car could be the key to tracing her."

I wasn't quite sure how it followed that the BMW could be key to tracking Gabriella down. The man from Cambridge who took me for Gabriella in the supermarket car park distinctly heard me addressed as Angelina. Furthermore, he was assured by my neighbour that I was no gardening expert.

"Richard," I said, "Please don't think I'm being argumentative, but I really can't see any reason not to take the BMW out. Dunoon's not that big a place. If someone really was in town looking for Gabriella, and we agree it's a big if, it wouldn't be difficult to spot her whether we take the car out or not."

"Ah, I'm sorry I didn't make myself clear. We need to make sure Gabriella isn't spotted at all. With regard to the car, I just assumed you might decide to go for a drive together and if your acquaintance from Cambridge happened to be around, he might notice a second person in the car who looks very like you. Gabriella would certainly want to use the car to go shopping. We know she isn't over-fond of walking."

"I hadn't thought of that," I conceded. "Yes, you're right, we'd better leave the BMW in the garage."

"What I'm thinking, is that it doesn't matter if you're seen about town, as you live in Dunoon. People know you and there are plenty like your neighbour Jean what's-her-name who will verify who you are. But please, as a precaution, make sure that Gabriella stays in the house from now on. If there's shopping to be done, you go by yourself. Tell her to stay away from the windows too."

"I don't think she's going to like that at all."

"I agree. I'll tell you what, let me see if I can reach George and get him to call her. She's more likely to listen to him than to either of us. By the way, the BMW is in the garage isn't it? Not out on the driveway?"

"Oh yes," I reassured him. "And the garage is locked. We won't take it out, Richard, I promise."

"Good. You'll be rid of it soon. I'll try to have your Mini sent up to you before I finish here. Otherwise, like I said, I'll drive it up myself sometime next week."

Gabriella predictably was not at all pleased when I relayed my conversation with Richard. She was enjoying driving the BMW and had been planning to do some work in my garden during her visit. I wasn't terribly worried. Gabriella might mutter and complain about her confinement, but she has plenty of common sense and I thought she could be relied on to heed Richard's advice. A back up call from George wouldn't hurt though.

Summer evenings stay lighter up here in Scotland than further south, and Gabriella, either forgetting or ignoring Richard's admonishment to keep away from the windows, was enjoying watching about thirty eider ducks fishing along the shore from my living room window. The shore road runs between the Clyde Estuary and my house and the tide washes in almost to the road, so we are able to watch lots of coastal bird life directly through the window, particularly gulls, ducks, and oyster catchers, swans, heron and gannets.

"Aggie," she called to me from the window, "didn't you tell me it was a grey VW Golf that followed us into the car park this afternoon? You know, the one with the driver from Cambridge who thought you were me?"

"Yes, it was, why?"

"Well, a grey Golf's just gone along the road in front of the house. It may not be the same one, but I had a feeling the driver was looking at the house. Now I know you're going to ask if I moved back from the window before he could see me because I can read your mind."

She can't of course, but I let it go. "Which way was he going?" I asked.

"Towards town."

I joined Gabriella at the window. "He did tell me that he and his wife have been staying in a holiday lodge this last week," I reminded her. "And there's that large holiday park with lodges and caravans further up the road from here. If that's where he's staying, this is the way he'll come if he's going into town. He could be going back to the store for something he forgot earlier. They stay open 'til nine. Let's not get carried away, Gabs. This is the height of the holiday season and there are all kinds of cars coming and going. I wouldn't be a bit surprised if there are several visitors here driving grey Golfs. You can't assume you saw my man from Cambridge just because you saw that one drive past the house."

I started to move away from the window. "Hold on Aggie, come back."

Gabriella grabbed my shoulder. "No, stand back, here he is again. Look, he's coming back. I think it's the same car and yes, I can't be sure, but I think he's looking up at the house again."

It was true. A grey Golf was going past the house again, this time in the opposite direction, towards the holiday park. We were standing a few feet back from the window and the driver's face was hidden by the roof of the car so we really couldn't see whether he was looking towards the house or not. But, as we assured each other, if we couldn't see the driver, then it was unlikely that he could see us either. We knew that we were making unwarranted, maybe silly assumptions about the driver, but were the two grey Golf sightings really just coincidence?

Common sense said that we were both tired after our long journey from Bungay, so it was not surprising that our imaginations were on overdrive after my encounter at the supermarket that afternoon. Grey Golfs driving past the house in both directions within a couple of minutes of each other would not normally be worth mention. That evening though, the timing of the sightings, right after Richard's warning to keep Gabriella out of sight, spooked us. I immediately went round the house checking that all the doors and windows were locked and drew all the curtains. Then I made hot chocolate, just as we did when we were children after frightening each other with ghost stories.

14

The telephone rang during breakfast on Friday morning. I knew it wouldn't be Richard calling, because he calls my mobile, and since it was still only just after eight-thirty it was rather early for cold callers.

"George maybe?" I suggested to Gabriella. "It won't be Richard on the land line."

"I doubt it," she said, shrugging and taking another piece of toast. "He always calls my mobile too."

I got up from the table and picked up the receiver. As usual, I waited for the caller to identify themselves. There was silence at the other end of the line. The caller was waiting for me to speak first, but I didn't. Finally, a male voice asked, "Am I speaking to Dr Gabriella Chester?"

I recognised the voice.

"Is that Mr Jenkinson, the gentleman who called me yesterday?" I enquired, letting him know I recognised his voice, but purposely omitting the 'Professor' title. "No, this is not Dr Gabriella Chester." I put the receiver down firmly and turned to my sister.

Gabriella, overhearing, had gone pale.

"Are you sure it was the same man? The one who was claiming to be Cyril yesterday. You're quite sure it wasn't a soft voice with a Yorkshire accent?"

"No question of it, Gabs." I declared confidently,

"Same pompous voice and accent. By the way, did you notice I purposely called him 'Mr'?"

"Yes, I did. Why did you do that?"

"I was conveying the impression," I replied airily, "that I'm innocently unfamiliar with academic titles."

"You shouldn't bother, Aggie," she sighed. "You never were much good at acting."

Gabriella always was jealous of my ability to think on my feet.

Rising above my sister's cattiness, as I always do, being the older and more mature twin, I said, "Gabs, this is proof that Richard was right. Someone is very anxious to find you. They know by now that your research isn't on either of your computers. I know it's a long shot, but what if that man from Cambridge who waylaid me yesterday is the same one that's been phoning, claiming to be Cyril Jenkinson? What if it *is* him, and he really *was* looking at the house yesterday evening? And if so, how on earth did he find out where I live? I know the car wasn't followed when we drove home yesterday because I kept checking in the mirror to see."

"Well, I know you weren't convinced, but I'd take an oath that the driver of that grey Golf was looking up at the house last night. You know he could easily get your address from the telephone directory."

"No, he couldn't. I'm not listed."

"Well, I just bet there are ways on the web to match telephone numbers to addresses. Let me call George and ask. He'll know if it can be done."

Gabriella had left her mobile in her bedroom so went to get it. Meanwhile, I started to clear away the breakfast things. She came back into the kitchen a few minutes later saying she couldn't imagine where she had put the darned thing last night.

I noticed she was wearing one of my skirts, so suggested she might have left it in the pocket of the jeans she wore yesterday.

"I doubt it," he said. "But I'll go and look anyway." She went back to her room to check her jeans and came back waving her mobile.

"Yes, it was in my jeans pocket. Good idea to look there. Thanks."

I got on with the washing up while she fiddled with her mobile and put it to her ear a few times.

"There's no reply. That's really odd," she said, looking perturbed.

I was rather surprised that Gabriella was concerned at not getting through to George immediately. I said, "Gabs, you can't expect George to be there the minute you call. I often have to wait for Richard to return my calls when he's busy working. Do you normally get through to him straight away?"

Gabriella coloured and turned away quickly.

"Oh, well you see, um, well you see, um, it wasn't George that I was calling."

"Oh, sorry. It's just that you said you were going to call George before you went looking for your phone. I don't want you to think I'm prying, but who else would you be calling at this time of day?"

"Well, you see Aggie, it's just that Cyril and I often have a natter around eight-thirty. It's way past eight-thirty and he still hasn't called so I thought maybe I'd better call him. You know, just to make sure he's all right."

"Why, has he been ill or something?"

"No, of course he hasn't. He's in very good health, but Cyril and I are good friends and I … well, we're quite fond of each other."

Now this was a new twist, or maybe I missed something yesterday when Gabriella insisted that Cyril Jenkinson could not have had anything to do with the computer thefts at her house, because the Thames Estuary voice on the telephone was nothing like his north country accent. I'd noticed she was a bit flustered at the time but just assumed she hadn't liked the suggestion that a friend and colleague would take advantage of her. Now it seemed there was rather more to her friendship with this Cyril. Regular morning chats? Hmm!

"What am I going to do now?" Gabriella was obviously distressed, but I wasn't sure whether she was worried about Cyril not calling or upset by the events of the past two days. Maybe both were getting to her.

"Don't worry," I soothed. "Things will work out. They always do."

"You always say that and yes, I daresay they will, but in the meantime, what am I going to do?"

"Well…"

"What am I going to do, Aggie? I can't go into town. I can't work in the garden. You've no books worth reading in the house because you give them to charity shops when you've read them. What on earth am I going to do, cooped up here?"

Now this was much more like my sister. Gabriella always was peevish. I had a surprise for her though.

"I've something to show you. Follow me."

I led her to a door in the hallway that previously opened to a large coat closet and flung it open with a flourish. I waved my hand airily towards a newly installed stairway rising to a landing in the roof space.

"Ta-da! Come on, see if there's anything to interest you up here."

I led the way up to a large, airy room with skylights on all four slopes giving excellent lighting all round. Richard and I had painted the walls and ceiling ourselves, the ceiling white and the walls magnolia. We had chosen an oatmeal carpet. I noticed Gabriella looking thoughtfully round the room. Before she could say anything about our colour scheme, or lack thereof, I quickly pointed out that we were still in the process of converting the roof space into a quiet library-cum-hobbies room.

"As you can see, we haven't finished yet. We only have bookcases, recliner chairs and a table up here so far, but isn't it a lovely place to read or listen to music? This might be a good place for you to spend time while you're confined to the house, Gabs."

Gabriella gazed round the room a second time and declared, "It's perfect, and look, with those skylights, the lighting's perfect for painting! I'll tell you what, why don't you go into town and get me some art supplies and I can put my time to good use while I'm here."

I'll say this for Gabriella, she doesn't waste time once she sets her mind on doing something. I forced myself not to think of paint on the new carpet and promised to see what I could find in the way of art supplies.

You'd better write out a list for me," I told her. "Do it while I make coffee."

She followed me happily back downstairs and went straight to my office, where I heard her murmur dreamily to herself, "Cyril would love that room," as she rummaged through my stationery.

15

The doorbell rang. We looked at each other in horror. Gabriella scurried quickly upstairs into our new loft while I went to answer the door. It turned out to be just the postman delivering a parcel for Richard, but that ring of the doorbell after the earlier phone call really rattled us. I thanked the postman, locked the door carefully and called an all clear to Gabriella. The postman's visit gave me an idea though.

"You know what, Gabs, rather than have me go out and maybe get the wrong things – that's assuming I can find out where art supplies are available here – why don't you order everything you need online? That way you'll get exactly what you want. If you order right away, it should all arrive in a day or two. Just be sure to have them sent here, not to Bungay."

"Maybe it would be safer to have them sent to you, rather than to me."

"Good idea, but you'd better use my credit card if you're using my name and address. You can pay me back later."

"Thanks, Aggie. I'll do you a painting in return."

That was not exactly the kind of paying back I had in mind, but I let it go. Gabriella always was tight-fisted!

"I think I'll do a spot of gardening this morning," I said virtuously, thinking to demonstrate to my sister that I am not a total loss as a gardener. "I'm going to trim those shrubs over by the road. They're beginning to spread over the wall. They'll get in the way of passers-by if I don't cut them back."

"Are you sure you know how?" asked the expert derisively. "There is a proper technique, you know. Maybe you should just pay someone else to do it, as you usually do."

'Well Gabs, I shall hold one handle of my snippers in my right hand and the other handle in my left. Then at the appropriate juncture on each branch, I shall snip. Just remember, while I'm out in the garden, not to answer the doorbell or pick up the landline if it rings."

On this exit line, I marched out into the garden with my snippers, ignoring mutterings from the gardening expert condemned to stay indoors.

Snipping overgrown shoots and branches made my fingers ache after a series of tough cuts. It was never my favourite job in the first place. I originally planned to work my way along the low wall that separates my garden from the footpath along the coast road, but it was slow and scratchy work, much better left to someone with a power trimmer. After a virtuous half hour, I sat gratefully on the wall while I conjured up an iron-clad reason to stop and go back indoors. Every excuse I considered was open to derision from my sister.

Blunt snippers? … An obvious lie!

Midges? … Put on some jungle juice, you idiot!

Mustn't disturb the bees? … Bees aren't that easily disturbed!

Done all the snipping necessary for now? … Can't even see where you've snipped!

I was still pondering excuses when I became aware of a man on the footpath the other side of the wall. I was not surprised to see a stranger there because summer visitors do sometimes stop as they walk past and ask if they are going the right way for the holiday park. I turned, ready to be helpful.

The stranger hesitated, then blurted out, "You must … excuse me … please excuse me … but I believe you must be … actually I know you are because you are so alike…"

This stranger obviously knew Gabriella and knew her well enough to know she had a sister. He was of medium height, with a pleasant face and well-barbered grey hair, soft spoken and wearing a smart grey suit. But was he friend or foe? If he was a friend, I had a pretty good idea from the voice and northern accent whom I was talking to but let's not take risks. I had to play it cautiously.

"I'm sorry…"

"Please, you are Dr Angelina Maud, aren't you? There's no mistaking your likeness to Dr Chester. Don't be alarmed, it's just that I need to get in touch with her. Seriously, I'm very worried about her. Could we possibly go somewhere less public to talk?"

I still needed to be certain before revealing Gabriella's whereabouts, so I hesitated to take him into the house. After all, the stranger at the supermarket had sounded perfectly plausible too.

"Well," I conceded, "if you just shinny over the wall, we can go round to the other side of the house away from the main road, then you can tell me who you are and why you're here."

I led him past the bushes, across the lawn and round to the less exposed front of the house which faces onto our access road.

"Please, I beg of you," he urged, "just tell me, is your sister here with you?"

"First, tell me who you are and why..."

At this point the front door was flung open and Gabriella burst out. She wrapped her arms around the stranger, laughing and sobbing, "Cyril, oh Cyril! I saw you through the window just now. I've been trying to reach you. I've been so worried something might have happened to you!"

"Not nearly as worried as I've been about you, my love. Thank goodness you're safe here with your sister."

My love? Safe here with your sister?

I eased the pair of them, still entwined round each other, into the house, closed the door and once again locked it firmly. Gabriella and the stranger, now confirmed as Cyril Jenkinson, just stood there in the hallway gazing soppily at each other. There was only one thing to do.

"Take him into the living room," I instructed, "while I go and put on a pot of coffee. By the way, Dr Jenkinson..."

"Oh please, Cyril."

"All right, Cyril, would you like something to eat with your coffee? Cake, biscuits?"

"Wonderful. Anything at all," he replied eagerly.

Gabriella picked up immediately, "Cyril, love, are you hungry? When did you last eat?"

"I bought a Mars bar and a packet of cheese biscuits at the train station. Oh Gabby, it's wonderful to be here with you and to know you're safe."

"Look, Cyril," I said firmly, "we need to sort out exactly what's going on. Right now, Gabby mustn't be seen. We're not sure who's looking for her but maybe you can shed some light there. Meantime, you're welcome to stay in this house as long as you keep indoors, out of sight. Don't answer the door or telephone. Just wait until I get coffee and biscuits for you, then you can tell us your side of the story and we'll tell ours. Don't start until I get back."

I unashamedly used instant coffee so as to be quicker, threw an unopened packet of biscuits onto the tray rather than put them out on a plate, and hurried back to the living room. I needn't have worried about missing anything though. Gabriella and Cyril were still busy reassuring each other that everything was all right.

When I reappeared with coffee and biscuits, Cyril, now settled comfortably on the sofa and still holding her hand, told us his story.

16

Everything began, he told us, when Professor Robert Smiley, the head of the horticulture department at the Institute had been scheduled to give a public lecture on the latest developments in composting. Composting was not his specialty, so he asked his faculty colleagues if they were aware of any current composting research he ought to include in the lecture. The name Dr Gabriella Chester came up several times in the discussion and he was advised to contact her. She had actually participated in a department seminar on composting a few months ago. Unfortunately, Professor Smiley had been attending a conference in the US at the time and so missed the seminar and missed meeting Gabriella.

Being a rather shy man, and having missed the seminar, Professor Smiley felt at a disadvantage and somewhat hesitant to approach Dr Chester himself, so on Thursday, he asked his colleagues if any of them felt they knew her well enough to do so on his behalf. Two colleagues volunteered: Cyril and another researcher, Michael Winter, who was one of a team working on pollination and polytunnel techniques. Cyril, the more senior of the two, was asked to contact Gabriella.

Composting was not a particularly hot topic for research in the Horticulture Department at all at

that time. Current interest had veered towards larger scale food growing methods in different parts of
the world. Cyril was in fact one of the few faculty
members who had taken much interest in Gabriella's
work. He suspected she could just possibly be on the
verge of a breakthrough with potential commercial
implications for home gardeners. However, they both
agreed she would need at least another year for rep-
lication tests to confirm her results. Nevertheless,
to oblige Professor Smiley he undertook to contact
Gabriella and sent the email immediately.

Gabriella's predictable reply that evening, that she
still needed to verify her experiments before sharing
her results, came as no surprise. It simply confirmed
what he already knew. He forwarded her email to
the Professor straight away and assumed that was
the end of the matter. He was wrong.

Michael Winter happened to be within earshot
on Friday morning when Professor Smiley read
Gabriella's email, and overheard his comments to
his secretary:

"It's a shame Dr Chester's not ready to tell us
more about the work she's doing, but if she needs
more time, then so be it. I'll still mention her in my
talk of course because her work is well known in the
community and I can say that we look forward to
getting her report when she has completed her current research. That should cover it."

On Monday afternoon Cyril filled his mug at
the department coffee machine and took it back to
his desk. Before settling down to the report he was

working on, he emailed Gabriella. The email bounced back just like the one he sent from home earlier that morning. He was about to telephone to let her know her email wasn't working when Michael Winter walked into his office carrying a small laptop.

"I need your help with something, Cyril," he said.

Cyril had always been willing to help his colleagues with their work. He looked up from his desk and smiled. "What can I do for you Michael?"

"Well," Michael Winter began hesitantly, "it's um, it's like this, Cyril. After Professor Smiley read the email from Dr Chester that you forwarded to him, he asked me to try to contact her again."

Disregarding Cyril's obvious surprise he continued, "A friend and I happened to be going near Bungay this weekend for a cycle rally, so I went to see Dr Chester. I thought she might be more willing to let us have an interim report on her research if I went and asked her in person. Anyway, after we explained why we needed it, she said her files are too big to send by email and she didn't have a spare external drive to put them on for us. She said it would take her too long to sort out which we need in any case. She suggested that we might like to borrow her laptop instead, select whatever we need, and transfer the data ourselves. We picked it up early this morning on the way here. I promised to return it of course."

Loan her laptop to perfect strangers? Never! Cyril was suspicious, concerned too. He knew Gabriella! She would never have handed her laptop over to anyone, let alone a complete stranger. Furthermore, he knew there would be no research files on the laptop. The first time he visited her house she had shown her system off to him very proudly. She kept the laptop on the kitchen table to be handy for correspondence, calendar and day-to-day business matters and used the larger desk computer in her office for research work. He knew too, that she kept duplicate data on external drives in her office.

Cyril did not share this information with Michael. He wanted to know what his colleague was up to. He decided to string him along and try to find out how he'd managed to persuade Gabriella to part with her laptop. He said casually, "Well done Michael! I'm surprised she lent you her laptop though. You must have made quite an impression on her."

"Yes, I must have," Michael Winter replied airily. "The only thing is, I forgot to ask for her password so can't get into the darned thing."

"Surely, you could just email her and ask for the password? Oh no, of course you couldn't, you have her laptop. Why don't you just telephone her?"

"Ah! Now that's where I need your help, Cyril. She must have an unlisted number. I don't see her name in the telephone directory. Still, I know she discusses her research with you so you're sure to have her number. Can I have it?"

That sounded more like a demand than a request.

"Sorry Michael, I don't have it here," Cyril lied. He nodded towards his office door, a clear signal to his colleague to leave.

The following morning Michael Winter came into Cyril's office again.

"Cyril, did you bring Dr Chester's phone number with you today?"

"Oh dear, you know what Michael, I forgot all about it. You know though, I emailed her last Thursday about her research, just as I said I would, and forwarded her reply to the Prof. She said clearly, in her reply, that her results still need to be confirmed and she needs more time before sharing them. That's why I was so surprised yesterday when you told me she lent you her laptop to look at her data. I'd say forget it."

"Cyril, I don't think you understand. This is a direct request from Professor Smiley."

"It makes no difference who requested her number if I don't have it, Michael," Cyril replied firmly, "Now please leave my office and let me get on with my work. Close the door as you go."

Michael Winter departed Cyril's office scowling. He left the door wide open to express his displeasure and marched back to his own desk in a cubicle across the corridor. Cyril heard him telephone someone. He could only make out the odd word, but Michael sounded very agitated.

Cyril couldn't understand why Gabriella had handed over her little laptop. He knew there would be nothing about her research on it. He badly wanted to telephone her himself to find out what was going on, but daren't make the call from his office and risk Michael overhearing and discovering he did in fact have her number. He tried to focus on his work but was interrupted by voices from across the corridor.

A technician from the polytunnel research team had joined Michael at his desk. Cyril could see the two of them studying some papers. The technician left after a short while, saying, "Sorry Michael, I'll get it corrected."

Almost immediately Cyril heard Michael's voice on the telephone again, this time even more agitated than previously. He strained to hear what was being said but could only catch a few words.

"...not left Bungay yet? ... must be ... yeah ... sure ... good man ..."

Cyril's concentration was completely broken. Who was Michael phoning in Bungay? He couldn't keep his mind on his work with one eye across the corridor and couldn't call Gabriella with Michael nearby. He decided to go and work at home. Remembering just in time that Gabriella's telephone number was written in his desk diary, he put the diary in his briefcase in case Michael should go searching for it once he was out of the office. He added some files to work on at home and put on his jacket.

Michael appeared again.

"Where are you going, Cyril?"

"I'm going to work at home, not that it's any of your business. If you want me for anything, I'm afraid you'll have to wait until tomorrow."

Cyril marched out of the building. He went straight to his car and tried to call Gabriella on his car phone. There was no reply. He tried calling her a second, then a third time but there was still no response. There was nothing he could do but try again later so he started his engine. As he approached the exit gate, he noticed Michael coming out of the building. He'd had enough of him for one day and didn't wait be pestered again so ignored him and drove off smartly. He decided to wait a while before trying to reach Gabriella again. He picked up a hamburger for lunch at a drive-in along the road, then called in at his local library to pick up a book he'd ordered. When he tried calling her again, there was still no reply.

When he eventually arrived home, he noticed Michael's car parked in his driveway. He slowed down for a better look. His colleague was standing at the front door. There could be no reason for Michael to come to his house other than to get Gabriella's telephone number and Cyril needed to check with her before handing that over. He also had a strong suspicion, in fact he felt ninety-nine percent certain, that Michael was acting on his own initiative rather than at the request of Professor Smiley — something else he needed to check out. The last thing he wanted right then was another encounter. He put his foot down on the accelerator and drove to a nearby car park, where he tried once again to call Gabriella. There was still no reply.

Since he was unable to reach her, he decided to call Professor Smiley instead. He needn't ask the Professor directly whether he had asked Michael to contact Gabriella. He could say that he hadn't

known that Gabriella's research was so important for the Professor's public lecture until Michael
told him he had contacted her. Decision made, he
tapped the Professor's number into his car phone.
Unfortunately, there was no reply from him either.

There was nothing Cyril could do until he managed to contact either Gabriella or Dr Smiley, so he
drove back home. Michael Winter's car was no longer
in the driveway, but he noticed the front door was
slightly open. He had locked it that morning when
he left for work and it was definitely closed when he
saw Michael ringing the doorbell.

He leapt out of his car and rushed through the
open door shouting, "Who's there? Is someone in
my house?"

Silence. He shouted again. "Is anyone there?"

Still silence.

The door from the hallway to the kitchen was
also wide open and through the kitchen he could
see that the back door, which opened into the kitch-
en, was wide open too. Glass shards from one of the
panes in the door lay on the floor. The key was still
in the lock, as it had been when he checked before
leaving for work. The door frame and the lock were
undamaged so presumably the key had been turned
by a hand extended through the broken pane. Cyril
rushed back to check the front door. That too was
undamaged. The intruder, presumably Michael,
had broken into the house through the back door,
but then left by unlocking the front door from
the inside.

He went straight to the front room which he used as a study. Inside the room he found his desk computer switched on. There was no sign of damage but could see that his study had been searched. The desk drawer and the top drawer of his filing cabinet were open, and papers spread on his desk, including personal correspondence. He had no doubt who had done it. Michael must be desperate to get his hands on Gabriella's research. He tried again to call her. If only he could find out what was going on. She must be somewhere where there was little or no signal for her mobile. He knew she would never have ignored his calls. He did not sleep well that night.

On Wednesday morning Cyril was still feeling shattered by Tuesday's events. He still hadn't been able to reach Gabriella. Michael would have found her number when he broke into the house yesterday. Doubtless, he would be having no success getting through to her either. Cyril couldn't face going into the office and having to deal with the man again. He called Professor Smiley's number. A secretary informed him that the Professor would be out of the office for the rest of the week. So much for that. He spent some time arranging to have his back door windowpane replaced. He would present Michael with the bill at the appropriate time. His mind still churned, and he managed to do very little work for the rest of the day. He was still unable to call Gabriella.

She did not respond to his calls on Thursday morning either. By now he was sick with worry. He went over the last week's events in his mind. Michael had said she had lent the laptop willingly, but had he threatened her? She had parted with her laptop, knowing full well he would find nothing on it. Maybe she had gone into hiding in case he came back again. If so, where would she be likely to go?

He knew she had a sister in Scotland, in Dunoon in fact. Yes, that was a definite possibility. Gabriella had said that the two of them were very close. Unfortunately, there was no easy way to look up the sister's telephone number. He thought her name was something like Angelina Maud, possibly with an 'e' but that's as much as he knew about her.

But Cyril could be resourceful when motivated. On the spur of the moment, he drove to the railway station, parked his car, got the next train to London and a West Coast mainline train from Euston Station to Glasgow. There was plenty of time on the journey to consult the web on how get to Dunoon from there. Once in Dunoon, he should be able locate the where-abouts of a Dr Maud fairly easily.

The journey went as planned, but by the time he got to Glasgow he reckoned it was too late to contin-ue on to Dunoon, so stayed overnight in a hotel.

17

Gabriella and I listened in amazement.

"Well, Cyril," I shook my head, "that's quite a story. It all ties in with Gabriella's experience. You were quite right in thinking she didn't part with her laptop computer willingly. Two men broke in early Monday morning and took it. Then, when they found there was no compost data on the laptop, someone came back on Tuesday and took her desk computer too. That has no data on it either because Gabriella cleaned it off after the laptop was taken. My husband suggested we should leave Bungay immediately, because whoever had taken the computers would come back again to question Gabriella, when they found nothing on the desk computer either."

Cyril was aghast. He had been unaware of either break-in at Gabriella's house or the fact that the thieves now had her desktop computer as well as the laptop. His eyes widened when we told him about our subsequent getaway from Bungay.

"I do hope you didn't tell anyone you were coming here," I added."

"Of course he didn't tell anyone, Aggie! Cyril's not stupid you know," Gabriella said, immediately leaping to his defence. "How could you even ask such a thing?"

"I'm asking," I said firmly, "because if anyone knows Cyril came here, you and your research files are no longer safe, Gabs. That's why!"

"Not safe?" Cyril seemed puzzled. "Oh, surely not. But Gabby, don't worry, of course I didn't tell anyone. No one even knows I left Cambridge. I just came here on the spur of the moment looking for you because your email isn't working, and I hadn't been able to reach you by phone all week. I was really worried about you. Then I remembered you telling me you sometimes visit your sister. Also, though, I wanted to warn you about Michael Winter. He seemed pretty desperate to get his hands on your research and he was pestering me for your telephone number. I suspect he thought that getting your data was a good way to ingratiate himself with Dr Smiley, hoping for promotion in the next department reshuffle. Anyway, he won't be needing your research once the boss has delivered his lecture, so I suggest we spend some time together in Scotland until then. I have to ask though, love, why didn't you answer your phone?"

"Cyril," Gabriella said weakly, "you'd better hear the rest of the story."

"Is there more? Well, why don't the two of us go for a walk along the sea-front while you tell me about it."

"No!" I practically screeched. "You can't go outside, either of you. I just hope nobody saw you coming here, Cyril. How did you get here, by the way?"

Cyril smiled happily. "Oh, quite easily really. I left my car at the station in Cambridge, took a train to

London, then another one to Glasgow yesterday. This morning I took another train to Gourock and came across to Dunoon on an awfully bouncy ferry. Then I took a taxi here."

How could this man be so unaware? Did he not grasp the fact that Gabriella was in serious trouble, possibly danger? She had asserted that he was not stupid, but I felt the jury was still out on that.

"How did you know my address?".

"I didn't, but he taxi driver knew. Elementary, my dear Aggie!"

"My name is Angelina!" I snapped.

"I'm so sorry, Angelina," he said with what sounded to me like very false penitence. I couldn't be sure because he turned his head away so I couldn't see his face. "It's just that Gabby always referred to you as Aggie. I'll certainly stick to 'Angelina' in future. Anyway, why shouldn't Gabby and I to go outside? It seems a pity to stay indoors on a lovely day like this. Just look out of the window at that sunshine. Gabby looks as though she could do with some fresh air too, don't you love?"

Was he for real? Did it not occur to this man that Gabriella must have been scared out of her wits when her laptop was stolen? Did he not understand that it was Gabriella, not Cyril Jenkinson, who was the centre of the drama? He hadn't even asked her side of the story before wanting to go out for a walk!

I felt an elbow jab into my left side. My sister, who had stayed unusually quiet throughout the exchange, now said with a sort of conspiratorial smile, "Aggie, why don't I take Cyril upstairs and tell him all that's been happening and explain why we have to stay indoors. You could have a cup of tea ready for when we come back downstairs."

She nudged me again and made an attempt at a wink just to make sure I got the message. She was never any good at winks. Anyway, it dawned on me that she was wanting to be alone with Cyril. Don't ask me why. But of course, Gabriella never was one to miss out on an opportunity. Anyway, I got the message. It belatedly dawned on me, that Cyril had been angling to be alone with her too, when he'd suggested they would both benefit from fresh air. It had been a less than subtle hint. I took a deep breath.

"Good idea Gabs," I allowed, "Take Cyril upstairs. You'll tell the story much better than I could. I'll make the tea and rustle up some biscuits in the meantime."

The tea was stone cold by the time they came downstairs again.

Richard arrived home unexpectedly that evening. Now that was serendipity! I was already fed up with playing gooseberry to Gabriella and Cyril. Actually, it was Scrabble that the three of us played but it felt like gooseberry. I quickly introduced Cyril, then pulled Richard into the kitchen to explain what was going on, leaving the other two to play Scrabble by themselves. Somehow, I doubt they even noticed we were gone. Richard had picked up on the nuances immediately and was highly amused to find that Gabriella had a boyfriend.

"Well, sweetheart," he laughed, "you can have me all to yourself now! No more competition from your sister!"

I sighed, remembering the time last year when Gabriella had made quite a play for Richard, but then she always was a flirt.

While Richard munched on the remains of the vegetarian dinner Gabriella and Cyril prepared for the three of us, spinach salad with crusty bread followed by fruit salad, I brought him up to date with all that had happened since he telephoned the previous evening, including all we had learned from Cyril.

"He had no idea there was any more to the story than what went on at the Agriculture Institute. He actually came up here desperately looking for Gabriella. It seems they phone each other a lot during the week while she's in Bungay and he's in Cambridge Her mobile was switched off per your instructions and, as you know, her email wasn't working. We think he should stay here until the Professor has delivered his lecture and the hunt for Gabby's research data is over. What do you think?"

"You may be right, although I think there could be more to it than the lecture," he said seriously, "but go on."

"Well," I continued, "in any case, neither of them can go out of the house in case the driver of that grey Golf is on the lookout for them. We figure that by now he may be looking for Cyril too."

As ever, Richard was very practical.

"What sleeping arrangements do you have in mind if we're to confine both your sister and this Cyril fellow to the house?"

That was something I had been wondering about myself, having made one of the three bedrooms into an office.

"I'll tell you what," he said, "why don't you tell Gabriella that I'm very tired and we're going to have an early night. Tell her you're going to have to leave their sleeping arrangements to her. Show her the linen cupboard and tell her she can put her friend Cyril wherever she likes. It's entirely up to her. We'll just disappear into our room and leave them to it."

"Good thinking!" I said.

Richard carried his overnight bag into our room. I called Gabriella into the kitchen on the pretext of showing her where to find hot chocolate etc. in case they wanted a bedtime drink, and relayed Richard's suggestion.

"Are you sure you mean that Aggie?" Gabriella's face was pink; she always did blush easily. "You really don't mind where Cyril sleeps?"

"Upstairs, downstairs, in my lady's chamber — it's up to you," I assured her and went straight to our room.

Richard looked at me quizzically.

"Don't ask," I said.

18

At the breakfast table next morning Cyril had a suggestion, "I've been thinking, Angelina. It might be a good idea to get Gabby away from here in case anyone comes snooping. Why don't she and I rent a car and drive up to Inverness? No one would think of looking for us that far north, and we'd be out of your hair."

"Yes," added Gabriella happily. They had obviously been discussing this. "We could do all the tourist things like looking for the Loch Ness Monster. What do you think, Aggie?",

"Bad idea," Richard interjected before I could reply. "Think it through."

"Oh Richard!" Gabriella was crestfallen. "No one would think of looking for us up there. In any case, both Cyril and I would watch carefully for anyone taking an interest in us. Wouldn't we, Cyril?"

Cyril however had picked up on Richard's tone.

"When you say 'bad idea' Richard," he asked, "what do you mean? Do you really think Gabby and I might be in some kind of danger? After all, we're only talking about her research notes."

Gabriella didn't look too pleased at Cyril's casual reference to her work.

"What I'm suggesting," Richard said, noticing her reaction and hastening to intervene, "is that if you and Gabriella go to Inverness, or anywhere else for that matter, you would leave a trail. You'd be renting a car, buying petrol, staying in hotels, eating in restaurants, even buying a ice cream cone. Anyone looking for you would have no difficulty tracking you down."

"I take your point, Richard, I really do, but surely a few notes on compost formulae are hardly worth anyone chasing us all over Scotland for. As soon as Professor Smiley has given his lecture, Michael Winter will have no reason to look for Gabby any longer. He's only trying to score points with the boss, you know. He just sees it as an opportunity for his own career advancement."

I couldn't believe what I was hearing. How could a senior academician, who had been told of the break-ins in at Gabriella's house in Bungay and our subsequent escape up to Scotland, be so naive? Then I noticed Gabriella had gone quiet and her face was quite pink. Why, I wondered? Then the penny dropped.

"Gabby," I said quietly, "you haven't told Cyril all that happened in Bungay yet, have you?"

Gabriella's pink became bright red, "Well you see, we were actually very tired last night, far too tired to do much talking. I was going to tell Cyril all about it this morning."

Cyril had the grace to look embarrassed too.

"Why don't you tell me now," he said gently.

Gabriella sighed and began her story. She told him about the first break in at her house in Bungay when two men wearing balaclavas had taken her laptop from the kitchen. She had reported the theft to the police, who thought it was probably teenagers looking for something to sell. However, Cyril's earlier email concerning her data made her suspect the thieves were after her research records, presumably on the laptop, rather than the laptop itself.

Cyril nodded confirmation. "That's right, you emailed back to say you weren't quite ready to share it, as I knew you would. I passed your message on to Professor Smiley."

"There was nothing important on the laptop of course," Gabriella resumed. "It was all on my desk computer and backed up on data storage drives. Anyway, after the first break-in, I transferred all my research work to more backup drives, then erased it from the computer. I collected up my paper files too and stowed the lot in my car. Then I drove it to the garden centre and left it in the staff car park."

"Oh, that's all right then, you've got all your work safe. Well done! But where's your car now? Is it still at the garden centre?"

"Well yes, the car's still there, but my files are safe here."

"I don't understand."

Gabriella looked even more flustered but carried on. "Well, you see, Cyril, there's actually more to the story. Aggie drove down to Bungay for a visit and while we out the next morning the house was broken into again and this time my desk computer was taken."

"You're telling me there was a second break in at your house?"

"Yes. Anyway, when Aggie called Richard to tell him about it he told us to go to the garden centre immediately and transfer all my data from my car into Aggie's, then we had to leave Bungay immediately without even going back home. And Cyril, as we left the car park, there was another car turning in with two men in it. I'm pretty sure we were only just in time to get my data away."

"Well, you did, thank goodness!" Cyril was obviously relieved. "I'm so glad Richard told you to come up here. It saved me the job of persuading you."

It was clear that Cyril still did not appreciate the seriousness of the situation. Of course, he didn't know anything about Richard's background at that time but still …

"Actually Cyril," I intervened, "the story didn't end when we left the garden centre in my Mini. We were followed but managed to hide in a friend's garden until Gabriella's son George organised our getaway. He provided us with a different car to drive up here in case my car was recognised."

I outlined our rescue from Bungay via Cambridge.

Cyril stared at us, "Really? This is incredible! Oh Gabs, I'm so sorry, I had no idea. When I saw Michael with your laptop in the department, I guessed you hadn't given him it just for the asking, but I assumed he must have applied some kind of moral pressure. You know, appealed to your sense of collegial duty to help Professor Smiley out. Oh, how can I have been so stupid?"

Having by that time spent some hours in Cyril's company, I considered that a rhetorical question. He hadn't even asked about George's involvement.

"Well," he conceded, "I can see that we should keep a low profile, but I'm sure it would be all right to take a stroll along the sea-front here, just like any other holiday-maker."

I put my hands to my head. Fortunately, Gabriella intervened before I could say something I might regret.

"Actually Cyril, that might not be a good idea either." She explained how I had been mistaken for 'Dr Chester' at the supermarket and how she and I had gone to bed early that evening because we were so spooked by a grey car driving past the house.

That last addition to the saga was news to Richard too.

"That clinches the argument," he said. "Let's all agree then that Gabriella and Cyril continue to stay indoors out of sight, well away from the windows, until we know for certain what's going on."

He turned to me and raised his eyebrows, "Do you have any appointments or commitments for the next few days?"

I sensed what was coming next. "Nothing at all," I said, "other than shopping for groceries now that there are four of us."

"Right," he said. "Here's my suggestion. Angelina will go to the grocery store and get in adequate food supplies. When she gets back, she and I will be the ones to go off for a few days, leaving the two of you here. You'll have the whole house to yourselves."

Gabriella and Cyril looked each other as though they couldn't believe their luck.

"There is one condition though," he added, and Gabriella and Cyril had the grace to look serious. "If by any remote chance this house is being watched…"

He looked questioningly at both Gabriella and I and waited for our response.

"It is possible," Gabriella conceded. "Remember the grey car, Aggie?"

"Well,' he continued, if the house really is being watched, Angelina and I will be seen leaving, so it must continue to look empty while we're gone. OK?"

We all nodded.

"That means no going outdoors, keep well away from windows, no answering the door, no answering the house phone, no TV or anything that might show a flicker of light from inside the house, no closing curtains in the evening and no lights on even when it gets dark. Is that something you can agree to?"

Gabriella and Cyril both responded enthusiastically.

Richard nodded, "Fine then, we'll throw a cover over the BMW in the garage and take Angelina's Mini. I brought it back yesterday."

"Anything you want to add to my shopping list before I go?" I called to their retreating backs halfway up the stairs. There was no response. "Right," I said, "I'm off."

By the time I got back with enough provisions to last Gabriella and Cyril for a week, Richard had planned our itinerary. We were to drive in a clockwise circle up the west coast of Scotland through Fort William and on to Loch Ness, where I would be handed binoculars to look for Nessie.

19

"You were looking in the driving mirror rather a lot on the way here, Richard," I commented as he backed into a space in the car park in Fort William. "Were you just being cautious, or did you suspect we were being followed?"

"Yes and no," he smiled. "I kept checking because I was hoping we would be followed. Then we'd know for certain if there was anything in the grey Golf story. You know, the one that drove past your house and spooked you and your sister."

"And were we followed?"

"There was a grey car that seemed to be keeping pace with us for a while, but grey cars are common enough. It could have been coincidence. In any case we lost them half an hour ago. Do you want lunch?"

"I'm more peckish than hungry," I said. "What about you?"

"Let's see what's available along the main street. It's a bit up the hill from the car park but it'll do us good to stretch our legs."

Fort William attracts lots of visitors and the main street was thronged with people. We walked companionably among them, stopping to pick up a couple of sausage rolls, bags of crisps, bottles of fizzy water and some chocolate for a snack in the car. We hadn't done this for a while, and it felt good.

Back in the car, we debated our travel options. We planned to stay overnight in Inverness, so of course we would have to look out for Nessie as we drove along Loch Ness. Everyone knows there is no Nessie, but that wouldn't stop us looking.

Richard was about to start the engine when a grey VW Golf drove very slowly past us and parked two spaces further along.

"Did you see that!" I exclaimed. "Richard, did you see how that woman in the passenger seat looked into our car as they went past?"

"Yes, I did."

"I'm sure it's the car that drove past the house."

"Don't worry. If it is the same car, then we've done what we set out to do, haven't we? If they've followed us all this way, they think we're your sister and her boyfriend. Wasn't that the whole idea, to lure them away from Dunoon?"

"I suppose so, but when they realise we're not Gabriella and Cyril they'll — hold on a minute — I think she's coming to talk to us."

Sure enough, the woman from the grey Golf was striding purposefully towards us.

"Any idea who she is?" Richard asked.

I shook my head. "No one I know. Let's see what she wants."

The woman approached the car. I lowered my window.

"Dr Chester!" she cried happily, leaning down and

peering into the Mini. "I was so sure it was you. My husband wasn't in favour of stopping. In fact, he stayed in the car, but I just had to come and say hello. I do hope you don't mind. You see I heard..."

"I'm awfully sorry," I interrupted, "but actually I'm not Dr Chester. This is the second time I've been mistaken for her recently."

"You're not Dr Chester? I was so sure ... oh dear! Please accept my apologies, but I was so sure. You're looking puzzled, I'd better explain. You see, my husband and I are up here on holiday. Our home is in Cambridge. My husband is a scientist at the Agriculture Institute, just outside the city. A few weeks ago, we went to Norwich to hear a talk by Dr Chester on garden compost. It was fascinating. She showed slides of the results of different compost mixes in her own vegetable garden and flowerbeds. Unfortunately, we were unable to stay and talk with her afterwards, so I was just thrilled when I thought I recognised her here, but it seems I was wrong. I'm so sorry for the mistake."

"Please don't give it another thought," I said graciously. "As I said before, this is the second time I've been mistaken for Dr Chester."

Richard leaned over me towards the woman "Excuse me for interrupting, but my wife and I are just about to see if we can get a cup of tea at the hotel along the road. Maybe you and your husband would like to join us."

"Oh," the woman seemed uncertain. "That's very kind of you. I'm not sure. I'll have to ask my husband. He's waiting in the car."

She turned and hurried back to the Golf.

Richard said, "There's no question. They are following us. I was worried we might have got too far ahead of them on the road and lost them. They must have guessed we'd stop at Fort William. You know that woman couldn't possibly have seen clearly enough into the Mini to recognise you as they came into park. By the way, when you were hailed as Dr Chester at the supermarket back in Dunoon, how did you identify yourself?"

"I didn't. I didn't need to because Jean stopped as she drove into the car park to invite us to a birthday party for her husband next week. By the way, I told her we'd go. Anyway, she shouted 'Angelina' to get my attention. That sort of confirmed my name was not Gabriella."

"And you didn't tell him your surname or title?"

"No."

"Excellent. Here she comes, and I can see the driver getting out of their car too. Let's introduce ourselves simply as Richard and Angelina Carter, residents of Dunoon."

I nodded. We got out of the Mini and waited on the pavement. As the couple approached, the man stretched out his hand to greet me.

"Good afternoon, Dr Maud. We meet again."

Dr Maud? How did he know my name?

Richard quickly stepped in front of me, grasped the outstretched hand and shook it heartily.

"Good afternoon," he said. "I don't believe we've met. I'm Richard Carter. You must be the gentleman who also mistook my wife for a Dr Chester in Dunoon the other day. She may look very like this Dr Chester, but she is, as you have already discovered, Dr Maud. She's also my wife and entitled to be called Mrs Carter too."

"That's what I told my wife, but she insisted on checking for herself. You'll agree it's an easy mistake to make when I show you a picture of Dr Chester." He turned to his wife. "Do you have my mobile there dear?" He turned back to Richard, "We're using my mobile as a sat nav. My wife's in charge of directions. Anyway, let's introduce ourselves properly. We're Peter and Sylvia Parsons."

We all shook hands.

Sylvia took the mobile out of her pocket and showed me a photo of Gabriella's head and shoulders.

I nodded, "Yes, she really is very like me."

I handed it to Richard, who scrutinised the picture carefully.

"Yes, I can see why you thought my wife was Dr Chester. They're very alike. Is this a recent picture? I notice it's taken at some kind of party."

Peter Parsons hesitated. "Er, I didn't take the picture myself. A colleague from the Agriculture Institute emailed it to me. He looks after our dog when we're away. We do the same for him, of course. Anyway, when I called to check on Mollie, that's our dog, I mentioned seeing someone I mistakenly thought was Dr Chester in Dunoon. He said he was looking for her in connection with a lecture Professor Smiley is due to give and wondered if she is vacationing in Dunoon. He emailed this picture for me to check."

"Can I see the picture again please?" I gently took the mobile from Richard. "I'd like to have another look."

The picture had been taken at a dinner party, and Gabriella and Cyril appeared to be toasting each other. I saw my opportunity to deflect the conversation away from her.

"Who's the man sitting next to Dr Chester?" I asked casually.

Peter Parsons peered closely at the picture.

"Oh, that's Cyril Jenkinson. It seems he's missing too."

I noticed Sylvia kick her husband's ankle, surreptitiously but hard enough to get his attention.

"I mean," he added hastily, "my colleague, Michael Winter mentioned that Professor Smiley wants to talk to Dr Jenkinson as well as Dr Chester."

"Let me look at the picture again," Richard said. "Yes, it looks to me as though Dr Chester and this Cyril Jenkinson are attending a dinner together. It's just something in the way he's holding his glass up and looking at her, a sort of intimate gesture."

I took the mobile and looked again. "No question about it," I played along. "How romantic! If your dog sitter can't find either of them, maybe they've gone off somewhere together."

"I think they're a little old for that!" Peter Parsons sniffed.

"Oh, I don't know about that," I smiled back, "I'm sure romance can blossom at any age."

Sylvia frowned. "It's cold out here," she said. "Let's go and find that cup of tea."

"If you two don't mind," Richard interjected, "Angelina and I had better pass on that cup of tea. I've just realised the time. We need to set off for Inverness now. We've arranged to meet friends there."

I got into the Mini.

"By the way," Richard asked casually as he too got back into the car, "where are you two headed? Are you going back to Dunoon now or are you going to do more touring? I suppose it depends on how much time you have. You'll need to get back for your dog of course. Sylvia said you're from Cambridge. That's quite a drive from here. Will you break your journey somewhere?"

"Er, we hadn't really decided. Which way are...?"

Richard headed off the enquiry. "Tell you what folks, the A9 would be your quickest route south. Easy to take in Edinburgh that way if you have enough time. It's well worth a visit. Or maybe you've done Edinburgh already."

"Which way are...?"

"Angelina and me? We haven't decided beyond Inverness. Actually, we were discussing our options when Sylvia came to the car thinking Angelina was Dr Chester. Anyway, we enjoyed meeting you. Enjoy the rest of your holiday. Travel safely."

There was nothing the Parsons could do but return to their car.

"We're going to have a hard time shaking them off now," I said to Richard as we returned to the Mini. "I bet they stick to us like peanut butter."

"They'd better stick to us," he replied, "The whole idea is to keep them well away from Gabriella and Cyril until we can get to the bottom of what's going on. I don't think they're likely to give up after following us this far. I reckon that emailed photo of Gabriella that Peter Parsons showed us has convinced them you are Dr Chester, incognito. Let's just continue as though we don't know we're being followed, okay?"

"Makes sense to me. Let's get straight on to Inverness to meet those friends I mentioned to the Parsons. Do you know anyone in Inverness who might meet us at short notice?"

"I know a few people, but Jean McFee would be the most likely to be home. She keeps bees and sometimes has honey to sell. We could drop in at her place to see if she has any to spare at the moment."

"Excellent! Do you know how to find her place?"

"I'll give you directions."

"I've been thinking, it might not be a good idea to stay in Inverness after we've been to your friend's house for the honey. We don't want to meet the Parsons again quite so soon and there are plenty of places in Inverness where they could accidently bump into us again. They might even stay in the same hotel. We definitely want them to follow us, but we don't want them to get close enough to realise you're not the great Dr Chester after all. Peter Parsons already knows I'm not Cyril. I think we ought to carry on to Aberdeen today."

I nodded. If the Parsons started to talk to me about compost, they'd soon realise that I'm not Gabriella.

The next thing might be comments about how alike we are. I could just imagine Sylvia Parson exclaiming, 'Why, you could be her twin sister!'

"Yes," I agreed. "As soon as we've seen Jean and maybe picked up some honey, let's go straight on to Aberdeen."

So much for our original plan for a leisurely wander round Inverness. I picked up my phone and called Jean to check that she would be home and to let her know we were on our way for honey.

The Parsons' car was still parked as we set off. We honked and waved to make sure they could see which way we were going. Nessie would have to wait for another occasion.

20

Jean McPhee was an old friend from my Glasgow days. She taught all three of my children in primary school. We have stayed in touch over the years through a mutual interest in quilting. Neither of us had much time to pursue hobbies during our busy working years, but, like me, Jean took the opportunity to attend quilting events when possible and to purchase pieces of fabric in anticipation of using them someday. She is now involved in the regional quilting hierarchy so I meet her sometimes at quilting events.

She was delighted to welcome Richard and me. She showed us her sewing room, a veritable emporium of quilting paraphernalia, and took us to see her beehives and their related equipment. We purchased several jars of honey for our own use and to give away to friends. I knew that Gabriella in particular would be delighted with her share. Jean, a friend indeed, insisted we stay for a late lunch with her, and afterwards provided us with sandwiches, apples and water for our journey.

Thus fortified with food and supplied with honey to take home, we played something of a cat and mouse game with the Parsons *en route* to Aberdeen. We stopped in Nairn, parked, and went for a stroll along the beach. Sure enough, when we returned to the Mini, the Parsons' car was parked a short distance away. We pretended we hadn't seen them and drove off slowly, checking in the rear mirror to make sure they knew we were leaving. The Golf followed at a discreet distance. Approaching Elgin, Richard drove slowly and indicated well ahead that we were taking the road to Aberdeen via Huntly.

After the longish drive we were glad to park again and stretch our legs for half an hour in Huntly. On the way back, we spotted the Parsons examining the menu posted in the window of a restaurant along the main street They greeted us like long-lost friends and invited us to join them for a cup of tea. Richard thanked them, and said we were actually on the way back to our car. We needed to hit the road because we had arranged to eat with friends that evening in Aberdeen. I was thankful for his quick thinking. My pseudo identity as Gabriella would not have survived the close contact guaranteed by tea and cakes at a shared table.

There was nothing the Parsons could do except go into the restaurant without us. We couldn't be sure whether they would stay for that cup of tea or whether they would change their minds and leave as soon as we were out of sight and follow us. We hurried to the car.

"You know, Richard," I told him as we left Huntly, "I've been thinking. We might just as well have stayed in Inverness. I don't have any friends like Jean McPhee in Aberdeen that we can just drop in on, and it's going to be too late to drive straight on from Aberdeen to Dunoon tonight. The Parsons are just as likely to follow us to a hotel in Aberdeen as they were in Inverness."

"Well," he replied airily, "you're not the only one with friends. I contacted one of my ex-colleagues, Rory McFarlane before we left Dunoon. He lives in Aberdeen and said he'd be delighted to see us and even invited us to stay overnight with him. He's on his own now and hates the empty rooms. He wants to talk to me about downsizing. Anyway, I called him from Inverness while you were busy with your friend Jean and told him to expect us this evening. He gave me directions to his house. He said to come any time but warned me we'll be eating out because he doesn't cook. So long as we don't bump into the Parsons in the restaurant, we'll be OK. I'll call him now and let him know we're on the way and ask him to book a table so that we can eat as soon as we get there. You'll like Rory."

We didn't spot the Parsons in the rear-view mirror all the way to Aberdeen. The sat nav guided us to Rory's and we were able to park the car conveniently out of sight at the back. Rory was waiting for us and greeted Richard effusively. Imagine our surprise when he took one look at me and exclaimed:

"Ah, Dr Gabriella Chester, I've been asked to keep an eye out for you! What a coincidence! Hang on, I'll call Peter Parsons right away and give him the good news. He and his wife Sylvia are touring in Scotland and actually on the way to Aberdeen now. His wife is my cousin. I rarely get the chance to see them because they live in Cambridge. They'll be staying overnight but there's plenty of room for you to stay as well. I'd already told them I'd take them out to dinner this evening, so that'll be a good opportunity to meet and get to know them. You'll like Sylvia and Peter. Let me call them now and let them know you'll be joining us. Sylvia's a keen gardener so she'll enjoy having a natter with Dr Chester about gardening and whatnot. You and I can catch up on other things, Dick. What a wonderful coincidence!"

Wonderful coincidence indeed!

Richard put a restraining hand on Rory McFarlane's mobile before he could make good on his intention to call Peter Parsons.

"Hold on, Rory. Let me introduce my wife properly. I'd like you to meet Dr Angelina Maud, twin sister of Dr Gabriella Chester."

"Angelina please," I interjected. "Gabriella and I identical twins and often mistaken for one another."

Rory examined my face keenly, then fiddled with his mobile.

"There you are! Look!" He waved the little screen in front of us with a flourish, like a magician pulling a rabbit out of a hat. We both looked. Sure enough, it was the same photo the Parsons showed us back in Fort William.

"Peter forwarded this photo to me, Dick. I'd have been fooled if you hadn't explained your wife is a twin. They're remarkably alike. By the way, there's quite a connection between those two names, Angelina and Gabriella as well. I wonder..."

Before we could embark on further explanation, we heard the faint but unmistakable sound of car tyres on the gravel in front of the house.

"Ah, there they are. They called to say they were on the way. Now we can have fun telling them you're Dick's wife, Angelina, identical twin sister of Dr Gabriella Chester."

Richard grabbed Rory's shoulder and spoke urgently, "Rory, we're not here. Did you tell the Parsons you were bringing another couple to the restaurant?"

"Yes Dick, I did."

"Did you tell them who?"

"Yes, I told them they'd be meeting my old friend Dick Carter and his bride. Well, you haven't been married that all that long have you, and sorry Angelina, I didn't remember your name."

The doorbell rang. We both froze. Rory looked at Richard quizzically, "Is there something I should know Dick?

"Sorry about this Rory. I'll fill you in later, but if you don't mind, just take your relatives out for dinner as planned. Tell them your friends had car trouble back in Huntly and don't know whether they'll be able to make it to Aberdeen tonight. Where can we hide in case they come in?"

Rory pointed. "You can go right through to the back door and out that way."

"We'll be gone before you get back. Sorry about this, Rory."

The doorbell rang again. Richard and I scuttled

to a scullery at the back of the house while Rory went to answer the front door. We listened.

"Rory! Lovely to see you again."

"You too Sylvia, and Peter too of course. Now I hate to rush you, but we'll lose our table at the Crown if we don't get there within the next twenty minutes. Do you mind?"

"That's fine. We can go in my car; we're parked right here by the door. But what's the rush? What about those friends you mentioned? If they're meeting us at the restaurant, they'll be able to hold the table if we're late."

"Unfortunately not, Peter, so we need to get off now. It's a very popular eating place. The food's good you see. If you're not there on time, they just give the table to the next folks waiting in line. My friends may join us later. They phoned to say they had some kind of car trouble up near Huntly. Didn't you say you were coming from that direction too?"

It would have been helpful if we could have heard more, but Rory was shepherding the Parsons back to their car, out of earshot. We listened until we heard the car crunch away down Rory's gravel drive. As soon as they were safely away from the house, *en route* to the Crown Hotel, we drove off ourselves.

Richard and I spent the night in Stonehaven, some sixteen miles south of Aberdeen. We dined that evening on hamburgers and fries, topped off with an ice cream cone. It was not dinner at the Crown, but it was magic after our long day in the car.

We'd probably seen the last of the Parsons. Gabriella and Cyril were safe at home. Tomorrow, we would go home ourselves and once more peace would reign.

Faint hope!

21

The house looked deserted when we arrived back in Dunoon the following afternoon. That was good, of course. It meant that Gabriella and Cyril were playing their part according to plan. Richard and I called our greetings to them as we went into the house.

There was no reply. In fact, there was no sound from within the house at all, other than the clattering we made opening and closing the coat cupboard. That seemed even better. They were not supposed to respond to anyone at the door. I knew my sister would take every precaution to avoid being discovered in the house, but I had wondered about Cyril. My estimation of him rose a little. Just a little.

"Gabby, Cyril," I called.

No reply. Surely they recognised my voice. I called again, "Gabs, we're back."

All was silent. The house felt empty, but I was not concerned, confident there would be a reason Gabriella hadn't responded. I went upstairs to the roof retreat expecting to find them there, probably asleep in those comfortable lounger chairs that Gabriella likes so much.

They weren't upstairs either. No wonder the house had looked deserted when we returned. It *was* deserted! I went back downstairs to tell Richard.

He was busy on his mobile. I heard the name 'Parsons' at some point. Doubtless he would tell me what the call was about when he rang off. I put the kettle on for a cup of tea and sat down to wait for it to boil. I needed to tell him that Gabriella and Cyril were not in the house. I knew she would have left a note somewhere to say where they were, but I was tired and decided to have that cup of tea before searching for it. I must have dozed off because I was suddenly alerted by my own mobile ringing.

"Aggie, where are you?"

Gabriella sounded panicky. Now what?

"I'm home in Dunoon, Gabs, but more to the point, where are you?"

"I'm in Glasgow and I've lost Cyril. Oh Aggie, I don't know what to do."

I refrained from advising her what to do about that wimp, Cyril.

"Gabby," I said gently, "start again. How did you come to be in Glasgow?

"Well, it was Cyril's idea."

Of course it was Cyril's idea! My original assessment of him was spot on. For the second time I refrained from commenting, but Gabriella read my mind as identical twins often do.

"Oh, but Aggie," she protested, "it wasn't just Cyril. I was in full agreement."

I let that one go too. My sister can lie with the best.

"Fine Gabby, but why are you in Glasgow?"

"I had Cyril listen to that recorded message on your land-line from 'Cyril Jenkinson'. He said it was obviously Michael Winter and there's no problem. Michael's ambitious but basically harmless. My records are all safe in Dunoon and Cyril's here now to protect me. And, you know Aggie, we were just sick of being cooped up and needed to get out in the fresh air."

"I see, so caution to the wind!"

"Well, we knew we might be spotted walking in Dunoon, but we thought nobody would be looking for us in Glasgow. We covered ourselves up well with coats and hats from your cupboard and walked to the ferry. We went across as foot passengers and caught the bus to Glasgow at McInroy's Point. Before you ask, we were the only foot passengers on the ferry and no one else got on the Glasgow bus with us."

"What about the cars on the ferry?"

"Well, obviously we didn't want to draw attention to ourselves by wandering out on the car deck, so we stayed in the passenger lounge. Anyway, even if a car did follow us across the ferry and saw us waiting for the bus, they still wouldn't know where we got off."

Words failed me. Gabriella is normally both sensible and careful. Why on earth had she listened to Cyril, who so far had demonstrated neither attribute?"

"Where in Glasgow are you, Gabs?"

"I'm just outside the ticket office at Central Station. We decided to get the train back to Gourock instead of the bus. Cyril looked up the times. He says the train takes you right to the passenger ferry terminal at Gourock and a local bus meets the ferry at Dunoon."

"So when did he go missing?"

"That's the problem. I've been waiting for him for ages. I went to spend a penny and he said he'd get the tickets and wait for me by the ticket office."

"Maybe he needed to spend a penny too. How long have you been waiting?"

"More than half an hour."

"It's difficult to get lost at Central Station," I said, just managing not to add, 'even for Cyril'. "Have you tried phoning him?"

"That's the other problem. Cyril doesn't have his mobile with him. I have his as well as mine. You see, I put them both in my bag before setting off, so we couldn't forget to bring them, and then stupidly forgot to give Cyril his."

I took a deep breath. "Okay Gabs let's go over this again. You and Cyril arranged to meet at the ticket office at Central Station."

"Yes."

"Which ticket office?"

"What do you mean? Is there more than one? I'm outside a big ticket office here and there are taxis at the station entrance."

"Right, you're at the main ticket office. There's another, smaller one, along the side of the station near the Gordon Street entrance. You can get to it from inside the station or from the street. Cyril might be waiting for you there. Why don't you go along and see? Call me back and let me know."

"Oh Aggie! I do hope you're right. Oh, wait a minute, there's no need. I think I can see him coming now. Yes, here he comes! He must have realised there's more than one ticket office too."

Realised too? What a porky! She hadn't realised there was a second ticket office at all. She'd only just learned it from me. Maybe she and Cyril were well matched after all!

"We can get the train back now, Aggie. Cyril knows the way already of course. But he says we'd better get the bus home from the ferry in Dunoon instead of a taxi."

Now that was actually a bit of sense on Cyril's part. Maybe, just maybe, he wasn't completely daft.

"Right Gabs, good thinking. But we don't want you to be spotted getting off the bus outside my house, so here's what I'd like you to do."

"What?"

"First, when you get on the ferry, sit in the seats at the back so that you'll be some of the first to get off when you land. That way you'll be less exposed. Call me as soon as you're on the ferry, because I'll need to time to organise your pick-up at this end. Okay?"

"Will do."

"Now, there's often a bus waiting right at the ferry terminal in Dunoon. Get on it, but then get off again at the stop by the church in Argyll Street, the main shopping road. Walk up Argyll Street, past the traffic lights on John Street until you get to Queen Street where you'll see a Co-op supermarket on the corner on your right. You'll see steps from the main road going down into the Co-op car park. The Mini will be parked near to those steps. It will be unlocked, so both of you can get straight into the back. Hunker down and cover yourselves with the blanket I'm going to leave on the seat. I know it's going to be a tight squeeze, but it won't be for long. Call me when you're both well-hidden and I'll come and join you."

I admit that my plan was like something out of an old cloak and dagger comedy, but I couldn't think of anything better — and it worked! On the off chance of being under observation myself, I bought a few groceries from the Co-op and was idling conveniently near the entrance looking at a display when Gabriella called. I carried my shopping to the car, stowed it in the boot and drove the two of them safely home.

22

While I was dealing with Gabriella and Cyril in Glasgow, Richard was on the phone to Rory McFarlane. Rory had given him a lengthy account of his evening with Sylvia and Peter Parsons. The gist of Rory's account, according to Richard, was as follows:

While waiting for their dinner orders at the Crown Hotel, conversation naturally began with family news. This was soon exhausted, and Rory noticed Peter glancing at his watch. He felt this was a good time to introduce the topic he really wanted to hear about.

"So, Peter, how was your Highland tour?"

"Oh great! Thanks for asking. Yes, it was well worth going. The scenery was everything you promised. I'm just wondering though when your other guests are going to arrive."

"Well, you know what? I reckon the car problem must be worse than Dick thought. It may be something that has to wait until tomorrow to be fixed. If so, they'll have to stay in Huntly overnight. He hasn't called to let me know, but I dare say he will before long."

Peter didn't pursue the subject, so Rory conjectured that either he hadn't made the connection between 'Dick' and Richard Carter, or he was just too tired to care. Sylvia certainly looked sleepy. Rory was still very curious to know what was going on. Why were Dick and the lovely Angelina so desperate to avoid his cousins, so desperate, in fact, that they snuck out through the back door to avoid them. He had been looking forward to entertaining both couples that evening. As he told Richard, life was pretty quiet on his own.

A little later he reopened the topic more directly. "Tell me, Peter, what's your connection with this Dr Chester that you asked me to watch for?"

Peter perked up at the mention of Dr Chester. He explained that a friend of his at the Institute was helping his department chief, Professor Smiley, to prepare a lecture on composting. Michael had suggested the lecture should include Dr Chester's research. She was well known and rumoured to have developed an improved method of home composting, so her work would obviously add interest to the lecture. Professor Smiley agreed and asked him to contact her on his behalf. Michael had been unable to find Dr Chester and assumed she must be on holiday somewhere. He emailed his colleagues with the photo and asked them to help locate her.

The email arrived while the Parsons were staying in a holiday lodge in Dunoon. It was a couple of years since he and Sylvia had attended one of Dr Chester's gardening talks in Norwich. Had it not been for the photo Michael sent, he might never have noticed her. He assumed she was also on holiday in Dunoon. He introduced himself and said how much he and

Sylvia enjoyed her talk. She denied being Dr Chester and insisted she was simply a Dunoon resident. He assumed this was a polite way of telling him she wanted privacy while on vacation. Then another woman in the car park spoke to her, calling her 'Angelina'. This left him wondering whether he had made a mistake or whether she used a pseudonym at her second home in Dunoon, sort of incognito in her private life.

Peter relayed this information to his friend and suggested there might be someone else in the Horticulture Department who was sufficiently knowledgeable about compost to help Professor Smiley instead.

Michael said he had already thought of that and had tried to contact Cyril Jenkinson, instead. He had an interest in compost and appeared to be on friendly terms with Dr Chester. Unfortunately, he had been unable to locate Cyril either. That had led him to wonder if he and Dr Chester were together, travelling incognito so as not to start department gossip. He urged Peter to continue to keep an eye out for both of them.

Michael's suggestion of a romantic tryst between Cyril and Dr Chester seemed kind of doubtful to Peter, considering were both getting on a bit in years, but he agreed to continue watching for them. After all, Michael was looking after their dog while they were on vacation. It might add a bit of spice to their holiday for Sylvia too.

Rory could not imagine how Dr Chester's composting experience could be sufficiently important to Professor Smiley's lecture to warrant all this intrusion into her private life. If Peter's friend was so anxious to locate her, there had to be more to the story than Peter had been told. Hmm!

It was hardly surprising, Rory reasoned, that Michael and his colleagues did not know Dr Chester had a twin sister. There was no reason for them to know. He would never have known himself if he hadn't mistaken Dick's wife for her earlier that evening. He decided not to mention it to the Parsons though, because he intended to probe further.

Rory then wondered if he might get more information from Sylvia. He asked her casually whether there had been any more sightings of Dr Chester during their Highland tour. Sylvia was delighted to be asked. She had been left out of the conversation thus far and felt it was her turn. She told Rory, she had thoroughly enjoying playing detective, and she knew Peter had too, although he would never admit it. Michael Winter really convinced Peter that the woman he met at the supermarket in Dunoon was Dr Chester incognito. Of course, she and Peter were not actually watching for her after that, but they couldn't help noticing the house where she was staying and had noticed other figures in the house too.

Peter had kicked Sylvia's foot under the table, but to no avail. This was her moment. She told Rory how they set off on their tour and met Dr Chester again, quite by accident of course, in Fort William. She was traveling in a Mini with a man who said he was her husband. They introduced themselves as

Richard and Angelina. She and Peter had expected the male companion to be Dr Cyril Jenkinson, but he wasn't. She could tell from the photo, and in any case, Peter already knew what he looked like. The pair were sighted again along the road after they left Inverness and they actually met and talked to them again in Huntly.

Rory digested this information and asked when Professor Smiley was due to deliver his lecture. Both Peter and Sylvia looked blank. They had been so excited to recognise Dr Chester and then to be on the lookout for Dr Jenkinson too, that they hadn't thought to ask. They were just trying to help their friend, Michael.

Peter picked up on Rory's expression of concern as he listened to Sylvia. Michael's email request had seemed reasonable albeit unusual at the time. Thinking about it now though, when he reported back to Michael about that questionable encounter at the supermarket, with the woman he thought was Dr Chester, why was he asked to continue watching for her? And why was it so important to look out for Cyril Jenkinson too. Michael's request had seemed harmless the time. Now he began to wonder if he had been foolish to agree.

"You know, Sylvia," he said, "I'm beginning to think we might have gone a bit far chasing after those folks for Michael Winter. Whoever they are, they're just as entitled to enjoy their holiday in peace as we are. We should leave them alone from now on."

"Well, I don't think we're likely to see them again in any case if they're still in Huntly, because we need to set off for York tomorrow."

Rory raised his glass,

"Best of luck to them in Huntly!"

23

"So," Gabriella said when Richard relayed the gist of his call to Rory MacFarlane, "from what your friend in Aberdeen says, it looks as though the Parsons won't be coming back to Dunoon, so we can come out of hiding now,"

Cyril nodded happily. "I agree. In fact, I was never convinced that we needed to go into hiding in the first place. You didn't really think so either, did you, Gabs."

"Now just hold on for a minute," Richard said, "Rory didn't say they're not coming here. All we know is that the Parsons were in Aberdeen last night and that they have to get back to Cambridge. I agree, it's a good guess that they'll go straight on home from Aberdeen. They told us they were going via York so it would be quite a detour for them to come back to the west coast first. Nevertheless, let's just play safe a little longer while I put out some feelers."

Cyril looked puzzled. He hadn't been told the details of Richard and George's involvement in our escape from Bungay. Gabriella had sensibly maintained 'need to know' concerning her son's occupation and glossed over the details of our chase up to Scotland.

"I'm not sure what the problem is Richard," he declared. "Nobody looked twice at Gabbie and me yesterday when we went to Glasgow. You know, all that squatting down under a blanket in the back of the Mini when we got back to Dunoon was extremely uncomfortable and completely unnecessary. We've just heard that the Parsons were simply enjoying a bit of innocent intrigue, egged on by Michael Winter. Everyone's had their fun and now it's over."

He turned to Gabriella for confirmation. "Right Gabs?"

Gabriella looked uncomfortable. I could tell she had reservations but didn't want to disagree with Cyril in front of Richard and me. But twins always help each other out. These twins do anyway.

I said quickly, "Look Cyril, I think you'd be right if the only reason Michael Winter wants to find Gabriella is to talk about her research on behalf of Professor Smiley"

Cyril nodded knowingly. "I'm sure it was."

"Cyril," I kept my voice level, "Gabriella's house was broken into twice. Each time, one of her computers was stolen. When we went to retrieve the data from the boot of her car, which she'd hidden at the garden centre, two men tracked us there and followed us leaving Bungay. Luckily, we managed to give them the slip and got safely to Dunoon. After that, I had an email and two telephone calls from an imposter, claiming to be you, wanting to locate Gabriella. We've since learned they came from Michael Winter. Michael also asked Peter Parsons to keep an eye out for us. He and Sylvia followed us on our Highland trip, hoping I was Gabriella. Isn't that enough?"

Gabriella nodded gratefully. "Aggie's right, Cyril. Professor Smiley wasn't planning to include my work in his lecture at all until it was suggested to him by his department staff, including you. There has to be another reason for Michael Winter wanting my data."

Cyril took Gabriella's hand. "Are you really serious about this, Gabs?"

"Yes, love, I am. I'm pretty sure he's interested in the possible commercial prospects but can't be sure. What do you think?"

"I have to admit that I haven't been thinking about it at all except in connection with the Smiley lecture. Not that I undervalue your work," he added hastily. "It's just that you need at least one more growing season, and very likely more, to replicate your experiments and validate the results."

"Yes, that's what I said in my email to you before my laptop was stolen."

Richard interjected, "Cyril, what if Gabriella's experiments were done on a much larger scale, say by a large fertiliser company?"

"Well of course a large company would have the resources to do much more comprehensive testing in a wide range of growing conditions all at the same time, which would speed the process. But I really doubt whether any of the fertiliser companies I know would want to make that kind of financial investment. There's a strong market for the commercial fertilisers they produce already."

"What we're seeing more and more," Richard said, "is large companies buying up starter companies, sometimes to continue to operate them but quite often to close down the competition."

"But Richard," Gabriella protested, "I'm not planning on starting a commercial operation at all. All I'm doing is helping my neighbours to get the best out of their gardens."

It was time to change the subject.

"How would it be, Richard," I suggested, "if Gabriella and Cyril take your car and go up north for a while. If they pay cash for everything, they won't leave a trail. If we go and get the cash for them, they won't be seen around town here."

"Sounds reasonable," he said.

I went off to the cash machine, pleased with my sensible solution. How could anything else go wrong now?

24

We waved the lovebirds off early the next morning with sighs of relief on our side and probably on theirs too. I called a gardening service and arranged for some serious clearing up to be done on my borders, before Gabriella returned to comment further on their neglect. Richard's excuse is that he's away a lot. I don't have an excuse.

Later that morning Richard was at the kitchen window with his binoculars, watching a submarine come in. I picked up mine and went to join him. I happened to glance down towards the water and the road below the house.

"Richard," I said, "there's a man on the footpath who's either lost or looking for somewhere. He's staring at his mobile."

Richard looked. "Yes, probably consulting his sat nav. Looks like he's come to Dunoon on business of some kind. He's wearing a suit. Nothing to do with us."

Well, he's going the wrong way if he has business in Dunoon."

"You could be right, but wait a minute, is he looking this way at the house? No, he's moving off. He's finally decided which way to go. Tell you what, how about we have a cup of strong coffee to celebrate having the place to ourselves again?"

"Sounds perfect."

Perfection was not to last. Even as the seductive aroma from Richard's highly technical coffee machine wafted towards us, the doorbell rang. I was about to go and see who was there, but Richard leapt up. "I'll answer it."

"It's OK," I said, "I can easily…"

"No, I'll go. You stay out of sight."

I retreated back into the living room, out of sight from the front door, ears pricked. Richard opened the door. He didn't greet the caller, which was unusual for him. Instead, he waited for whoever was there to speak first. To my horror I recognised the voice.

"Good morning sir, you must be Mr Maud."

Richard said nothing.

"I telephoned Mrs Maud a few days ago concerning a mutual friend."

Richard still didn't speak.

"Is your wife available?"

"Unfortunately, not."

"Oh, well perhaps you can help me. I'm trying to contact a colleague of mine, Dr Gabriella Chester. I was told she came to Dunoon to visit her friend, Mrs Maud."

"And you are?"

"Oh, I'm sorry, I should have introduced myself. The name is Winter. Michael Winter. I'm up in Scotland attending a conference in Glasgow. By the way, I have to say, this is a beautiful part of the country."

"We think so. Are you combining a holiday with your conference?"

"Er, maybe a couple of days. I thought I'd try to contact Mrs Maud while I'm up here. Is she likely to come back soon? I could wait."

"Unfortunately, not. Do you have other lines of enquiry?"

"No but thank you for your help. It was a long shot anyway."

"Ah well, at least you've seen Dunoon now. Where are you from Mr Winter?"

"Cambridge. I'm taking the opportunity to do a little sightseeing while I'm in Glasgow and thought I might catch Dr Chester in Dunoon if she happened to be here with Mrs. Maud."

"I see, and how long will you be staying in Glasgow?"

"I haven't decided yet. It depends. By the way, when…?"

"Well, enjoy your visit to Scotland, Mr Winter. I hope the weather holds for you. Good day."

Richard closed the door, politely but firmly. We stood a little way back from the window sipping our coffee, watching him leave. As we watched, the black clouds which had been gathering overhead released a heavy downpour on our unprotected visitor.

"Well," Richard said, "what a load of eyewash that was."

"Rain-wash now. He'll be soaked through. By the way, I noticed he didn't mention Cyril."

"No, he didn't, but of course it's Gabriella he's looking for. Cyril was just a means of getting to her."

"Richard, I think I'd better call and warn them

Michael Winter is in Dunoon. They may not have got very far yet." I dialled Gabriella's mobile,

"Aggie, oh Aggie," she sobbed.

"What's wrong, Gabs? Have you had an accident?"

"No."

"Then what's happened. Is Cyril all right?"

"No...yes...well..."

"Gabby, what's happened? Tell me."

"It's Cyril."

Of course it was Cyril! I put the phone on speaker so that Richard could hear the latest peccadillo.

"Gabby, what about Cyril? You haven't lost him again, have you?"

"No."

"What's wrong then?"

"He proposed."

"And?"

"I said 'No'. I told him I was too deep in compost right now to think about it. Aggie! Stop laughing! Stop it! It isn't funny."

"Sorry, it was just the image of you in a pile of garden muck."

Gabriella sniffed.

"Incidentally, where are you. How far have you driven?"

"I've just dropped Cyril at Glasgow Airport. He said if I think more about rotting plants than I do about him he might as well go back to Cambridge. I'm coming back to Dunoon."

Richard took the phone.

"Gabriella."

"Hello Richard. I expect you heard all that."

"Gabriella, call Cyril right away and tell him to come back."

"He was in a bit of a huff."

"I'm sure he was. Nevertheless, call him now and tell him he must come straight back to the car. You both need to get away from the airport right away. Michael Winter's around and looking for you. Ring off now and call him."

"What if he doesn't want to speak to me?"

"Are you planning on marrying Cyril or not?"

"Of course I'm going to marry him. He just took me by surprise."

"Call him and tell him so. Get him back to the car and call us back when he gets there. I'm ringing off now, Gabriella. Do it."

25

Gabriella did call back, although we had an anxious half hour waiting for the call. We learned later that Cyril was not far away at the time she called me. He was already having second thoughts, debating whether to go on home to Cambridge or whether to go back to the car, assuming the car was still at the airport. Gabriella's call decided it for him. The overjoyed swain returned, presumably with a hop, skip and a jump, to the car. Don't ask where the half hour went!

When they did finally call, I managed to suppress my reservations about Cyril and congratulated them warmly. Then I explained that Michael Winter had come to Dunoon looking for Gabriella and had already been to our house. Richard told him I was not available, implying that I was out somewhere, so he might well be watching for my return. He could even be watching cars coming off the ferry at Hunters Quay. They mustn't come back to Dunoon at present. I suggested the best plan would be to continue their Highland tour.

"But that's going the wrong way," Gabriella protested. "The Highland tour means going north and Greta Green is south, near the border. Yes Aggie, we've decided to get married at Gretna Green. Now

I can tell what you're thinking but that's what we've decided. Don't forget, I nearly lost Cyril less than an hour ago."

Words failed me. This was my, on the whole, level-headed sister. I handed the phone to Richard. "You talk to her, love. She's more likely to listen to sense coming from you."

"I heard that. Oh hello, Richard. I expect Aggie told you our plans."

"Yes, and congratulations to both of you!"

"Oh, thank you. I just wish Aggie was a bit more supportive."

"Your sister's very supportive, as I am. But we're also very concerned about Michael Winter coming all the way to Dunoon to find you."

"He'll never think of Gretna Green. He's much more likely to think I'm up in the Highlands if I'm not with you in Dunoon. That's where people go for Scottish scenery. You don't go to Gretna Green for scenery."

"Maybe you're right. What do you think, Cyril? I assume you're on speaker and heard everything."

"Actually, Richard, I wasn't really listening because while you were talking to Gabs, I googled Gretna Green. Did I miss much?"

Richard patiently reiterated our concern about Michael Winter being in Dunoon.

"So, obviously the two of you should keep away from Dunoon right now. Gabriella says you're off to Gretna Green to tie the knot. What did you learn about Gretna Green from Google?"

"Well, I've only had time to glance quickly at the information, but it seems you have to book the ceremony in advance and there's a lot of paperwork to be done and arrangements to be made. I gather it takes at least a month to get through it all. You can't just drop in and have the blacksmith marry you as Gabs first thought."

"So, what now?"

"What I'm thinking is that we should go to Gretna Green and see the place for ourselves. It will be much easier to sort out at our options when we really know what we're talking about. According to the web, there are lots of decisions to be made, even the type of ceremony we want. Then we'd have to set a date and book a room for the ceremony and make all the arrangements. I think it will be a lot easier to decide everything once we've seen the place."

"Fine, good idea. You'll be less likely to run into Michael Winter at Gretna Green than most places. After you've made your arrangements there, why don't you continue on south, maybe tour round the Lake District or the Yorkshire Dales for a few days?"

"We can certainly do that, but won't you be needing your car?"

"Not immediately. We still have Angelina's Mini. By the way, Cyril, I believe that Professor Smiley is due to deliver his lecture tomorrow."

"Oh, that's right, I'm afraid the date slipped my mind. Well, it's too late now for Michael Winter to get Gabby's data to him in time."

"It is indeed."

"Yet he's come to Dunoon, still looking for Gabs. Hmm, that's worrisome. It supports the idea that he has other plans for her data."

"That's exactly my concern, Cyril. Anyway, can you and Gabriella stay well clear of him while I sniff around a bit? I'll stay in touch."

"Yes, we can. Thanks, Richard, and by the way, thanks too for talking sense into Gabriella for me."

As soon as they rang off, I said to Richard, "Did you ever hear such arrogance? What did you think when Cyril thanked you for talking sense into Gabriella? He's the daft one."

Richard smiled. "You know, you and your sister are quite protective of each other when you're not being catty. But you're quite wrong about Cyril. He's very astute when he's not being soppy over your sister. Whose silly idea do you think Gretna Green was?"

26

Gabriella and Cyril went to Gretna Green as planned but Gabriella's initial rush of enthusiasm dwindled after Cyril's discovery that they couldn't just drive into the forge and have a cheerful blacksmith tie the knot for them. When they arrived there after a two-hour drive from Glasgow airport, they looked around the Old Forge area out of interest, but as tourists rather than prospective customers. Gabriella called to tell us they had changed their minds and decided it would be more appropriate to be married in Dunoon, where they had first declared their love for each other or in Cambridge where they would be living.

"And you two can be Best Man and Matron of Honour," she said happily.

Gabriella always was romantic!

We didn't hear from the happy couple again for a few days. Plans, Gabriella informed me, had changed. She and Cyril had been in the Lake District, per Richard's suggestion, but were now *en route* to Cambridge, rather than back to Dunoon. They had no option about this because both she and Cyril had received emails from Professor Smiley. Cyril's was a departmental email with only Cyril and Michael Winter on its distribution list. The one Gabriella received was to her alone. She said that as soon as we rang-off she would forward her email to me. Cyril would forward his to Richard. They wanted us to read them for ourselves so we would understand.

"Read Cyril's first," she directed, "Call us back when you've read them".

Institute of Agriculture
Department of Horticulture
Distribution: C. Jenkinson, M. Winter.

My secretary will contact you to confirm your
availability to discuss a compost research
proposal this coming Wednesday at 2pm,
in my office.
R. G. Smiley

Institute of Agriculture
Department of Horticulture

Dear Dr Chester,
I recently gave a public lecture on composting.
Prior to the lecture, knowing your reputation
in this field, I asked one of my colleagues,
Dr Jenkinson, to contact you. He forwarded
your email reply to me, indicating you need
more time for verification before sharing your
results. My lecture therefore contained no
reference to your work. Nevertheless, questions
from the audience were entirely in connection
with your findings.

I have since been contacted by an executive from a well-known fertiliser company who attended my lecture. He was surprised and impressed by the interest your compost research has generated in the public domain. He indicated his company would be prepared to consider a proposal from my department for funding to investigate further. This would involve a larger scale trial of your findings. I would like to put a proposal together with yourself and a member of my department as joint principal investigators.

Would it be possible for you to attend a meeting to discuss such a proposal in my office in the Horticulture Department at 2pm, this coming Wednesday? Please reply at your earliest convenience if this is agreeable to you. We can reschedule the date if necessary.

I am sending this to you by email as well as by letter post because my secretary has been unable to reach you by telephone. I apologise for the short notice.

Sincerely,
Professor R. G. Smiley

"Well," I said to Richard once I had caught my breath, "what do you make of that?"

"Like you, I'm amazed. You know, I'm really glad Gabriella has Cyril there with her. He's calm and level headed and has experience in putting together proposals for research funding. He'll make sure Gabriella's not side-lined once she has shared all her data with them."

"Could that happen?"

"Oh yes. We've already seen evidence in the theft of Gabriella's computers and the various attempts to locate Gabriella herself after they failed to find her data on either computer. Professor Smiley is obviously unaware of all that's been going on. If he had been, Michael Winter would not still be around, let alone invited to the meeting. Anyway, Cyril will know how to handle the situation."

Up until that time I had never thought of Cyril as either calm or level-headed. To be fair, my dealings with him had been in unusual circumstances. I had been too concerned about Gabriella to pay much attention to him. Maybe I should have been more perceptive. Hearing Richard's assessment of him now, made me wonder if I had been uncharitable in my judgement. I recalled how he handled Gabriella's stupid, knee-jerk reaction to his marriage proposal and engineered a reversal in short order. He had also guided my determined sister gently away from that zany Gretna Green idea. That must have been a real test of diplomacy. Yes, I was certainly glad that Cyril would be at the meeting with Professor Smiley to protect her interests.

"You know," Richard said, "I'm going to need my car next week and Gabriella and Cyril are driving straight on to Cambridge for this meeting. Why don't we fly down to collect it from them? We could take a flight to Stansted tomorrow then get the train to Cambridge."

"Great idea, let's do it!"

We called Gabriella to congratulate her on Professor Smiley's invitation and to let them know our plans. I told her we'd call them when we arrived in Cambridge.

27

We had not expected Michael Winter to be a fellow passenger on the flight to Stansted. Richard and I were already seated when he boarded. I was by the window and Richard in the aisle for the benefit of his long legs. I spotted him as he came on the plane and gave Richard a warning nudge. I turned my face to the window, held a magazine in front of me and contrived to remain unnoticed.

Michael didn't see us at first, his eyes focussed on seat numbers. He walked straight down the aisle, stowed his briefcase in the overhead bin and then, to my horror, settled into the aisle seat directly across from our row. He then noticed Richard in the opposite seat and recognised him immediately from their doorstep encounter. Richard responded to his warm greeting, agreeing with his remarks on the shortage of leg room etc. By the time we were airborne, the two of them were chatting companionably across the aisle. I wondered at first why Richard was bothering to talk to him, knowing Michael for the charlatan he was. The answer became clear as the conversation progressed. Richard was carefully teasing out information.

Michael proved to be fond of talking about himself. He was, he told Richard, a senior researcher in the Department of Horticulture at the Institute of Agriculture. He was on his way back to Cambridge to attend an important meeting on Wednesday with Professor Smiley, the head of the department.

Richard had, of course, already seen both Professor Smiley's email to Gabriella and the one sent to Cyril and Michael, so was interested in Michael's interpretation of the invitation. He didn't want to alert him by showing too much interest, so asked casually whether he had managed to locate Dr Chester. Michael shook his head and said he had not yet discovered her whereabouts but would certainly need to catch up with her at some point. Not immediately though, the Wednesday meeting was his immediate priority.

Without prompting, he then confided to Richard that Professor Smiley was getting a bit long in the tooth and, although it was not official, there was an expectation among the department staff that he would be announcing his retirement soon. Several members of the department, himself included, had discussed his replacement among themselves, with an eye to their own prospects when the position became vacant. In fact, he told Richard, he suspected that the purpose of the Wednesday meeting was to sound out potential candidates to succeed him. In response to Richard's question, he admitted he didn't know exactly how old the Professor was but knew he must be 'somewhere up there in years'.

The meeting with the Professor, he told Richard, had officially been called to discuss research into garden composting. This was not a high priority field of interest in the Horticulture department, mainly because it was not a subject likely to attract serious research funding. Funding, he explained, is the life blood of research. His suspicion therefore was that Professor Smiley had chosen composting as a topic for discussion simply in order to evaluate prospective candidates' approaches to research planning and organisation. Other factors would need to be considered of course in determining suitability for the position, but vision for the future of the department would be a critical one. He intended to demonstrate his own vision and foresight by suggesting that a compost research unit would be a useful addition to the department to enrich the student curriculum.

Richard nodded and asked if many candidates were being considered for the position. Michael Winter thought that so far there were only two strong contenders, himself and a rather dull sort of fellow, Cyril Jenkinson. Richard looked thoughtful and said that he expected the choice between equally qualified and experienced candidates might be difficult. Michael Winter straightened up in his seat and said haughtily that while Jenkinson admittedly had a doctorate and was already in charge of several research projects, he himself had the kind of vision, initiative and drive that was needed in the future.

Richard wished him well in his career advancement, then casually indicated me sitting next to him.

"By the way, you weren't able to meet my wife when you came to our house, hoping she could help locate Dr Gabriella Chester. This is my wife, Dr Maud. But from what you've told me today, you won't be needing her help any longer."

Michael Winter looked as though he had seen a ghost.

I smiled, said, "Good afternoon, Mr Winter," and returned to my magazine.

We left Michael at Stansted Airport. He went off the direction of the car park. We went to get a train.

Gabriella and Cyril were at the station to meet us when we arrived at Cambridge. Richard relayed his conversation with Michael Winter on the plane. Cyril scoffed at the idea of Professor Smiley retiring as just wishful thinking on Michaels' part, as was his idea that he might be in the running for the position.

I reminded Gabriella about her research files. When we unloaded them from the boot of the BMW George lent us to drive up from Bungay, we had hidden them in a cupboard upstairs for safety. I told her that unless she had another suggestion, I would pack them up carefully when I got back to Dunoon and mail them to her.

Not to worry, Gabriella assured me breezily, there was no need. She and Cyril had boxed all her data up neatly during their enforced incarceration in our house. It had been a simple matter to stow the boxes in the boot of Richard's car before they set off on the Highland tour that never came to pass. She said she hadn't wanted to risk leaving her data unguarded in our house while they were gone. It was safer to take it with them.

Such lack of trust! I refrained from comment. Why was Richard grinning?

Gabriella drove to a hotel in Cambridge, where she had booked a room for us. She said that she and Cyril would like to keep Richard's car another day. She needed to go home to Bungay for fresh clothes and something suitable to wear for the meeting with Professor Smiley. They would stay there overnight. In the morning, they would go to pick up her Audi from the garden centre and each of them drive a car back to Cambridge and return Richard's car. It was only after they left that I recalled Cyril telling us he left his car at the station when he set off to find Gabriella. Surely, they could have used his car to go to Bungay. That's my sister!

Richard and I were walking along the banks of the River Cam when Gabriella called again. I had not been expecting to hear from her again that day.

"Aggie! Aggie, you'll never guess!"

She was quite right; I had no idea.

"You'll never believe me!"

She was wrong about that though. After the last couple of weeks, nothing would surprise me.

"My computers are back!"

Did I say nothing would surprise me?

"Your computers are back? How on earth did they get back? Have they been damaged? Have you checked to see if they're working?"

"Yes, we found them plugged in just as they were before and both of them are just fine. Oh, and by the way, the front door and the door to my office have been repaired too."

"The doors have been repaired?"

"Aggie don't keep repeating what I say. Just listen."

Gabriella always was bossy.

'I'm listening," I said. "Hold on, let me put the phone on speaker for Richard to hear too."

'Well," Gabriella had her audience, "I didn't notice at first because we went in through the back door as usual and straight into the kitchen and saw my laptop there on the table, plugged in. Of course, we checked it out immediately, then went to see if the desk computer had been returned too, and it had."

And was that one working as well?"

"Yes, perfectly. Anyway, then I remembered the splintered front door jamb. I think it has been replaced. Anyway, the whole door has been repainted, not quite the same shade but close enough. I expect they couldn't get the exact match. It needed doing anyway. There's a new lock on my office door as well."

"Goodness! Have you any idea who could have done it?"

"Well, I thought at first that George must have had it done for me, just like he did that makeover in your house after it was damaged last summer."

"But now you think someone else took care of it?"

"Yes, you see Cyril noticed a jacket hanging on the back of a chair in the kitchen. He's pretty sure it belongs to Jason Taylor, one of the lab technicians at the department. It has this very distinctive hand-embroidered cycle club badge on both sleeves."

"What are you going to do about it?"

"Oh, Cyril's got it all planned. When he goes into the office tomorrow, he's going to take Jason Taylor's jacket and hang it on one of the coat hooks. He says he won't need to do anything more than that. He reckons Jason isn't going to risk his job to save Michael Winters' skin and that as soon as he sees his jacket hanging there, he'll go straight to Cyril and tell all."

Cyril went up many more notches in my estimation after that. In fact, he stayed there.

I was told afterwards that his prophecy was correct. I would have liked to know the details, but Cyril wasn't saying any more.

28

Cyril brought Richard's car to our hotel the next morning, as arranged, and the three of us drove to the Agriculture Institute. Gabriella had not arrived when we got there, but Cyril said there was no need for us to wait, he would call her and tell her to go straight to his office. He wanted to go in and make a start on work that had accumulated during his absence. We should just go and enjoy our day.

As it happened, Gabriella's red Audi turned in to the car park as we were driving out. We stopped to say 'hi' and tell her that she had just missed Cyril going into the building. She looked a bit flustered, but I guessed that was probably due to traffic congestion. I suggested we meet for dinner that evening.

She nodded, "Right. Okay, Aggie, see you later. Look, we're blocking the entry, I'd better move on. Bye."

I was surprised when Gabriella rushed off like that, she was usually much chattier. She was right though; we were blocking the entry. We waved and drove off.

Half an hour later, Cyril phoned to ask if we'd heard from Gabriella. We told him we'd seen her go into the car park right after he'd gone into the building, and assumed she had gone straight to his office.

Had he tried phoning her? He said he had called several times, but she was not answering.

I tried calling her myself, with the same result.

Richard and I were not far from the Institute, so we turned and drove straight back to see if her car was still there. It was not difficult to pick out Gabriella's red Audi in the car park or to see that the boot was wide open. There was no sign of Gabriella though, or anyone else near the car.

"Oh no!" I exclaimed. "Gabriella, you idiot! I've been warning you about that for years. Now it's happened. Honestly Richard, it was bound to happen sooner or later."

"What's happened? What did you warn her about?"

Richard drove alongside Gabriella's Audi.

"Just look. She has this bee in her bonnet about leaving her car unlocked. She says she'd rather have thieves help themselves through an unlocked door than have an enormous repair bill if they force the door to get in."

The doors to the Audi were indeed unlocked, and no, there was no sign of damage inside. The open boot however was a different matter. The floor was a jumble of clothes with various boxes and bags upended and empty. I just hoped the clothes she said she was bringing for the Wednesday meeting were intact. The only things undisturbed appeared to be a large laundry detergent box and a large cylindrical porridge oats box. Surely Gabriella didn't think she needed to take detergent and porridge oats to Cambridge. Neither of them had asked for porridge for breakfast when they were in Dunoon, and as for detergent … she can still surprise me!

"Well," I said to Richard, "it looks as though the search is still on for Gabriella's data after all."

"Could be, although I'd have thought it unlikely. I hope she didn't have the stuff that she and Cyril boxed up in Dunoon with her today. If she did, and if that's what someone was looking for, chances are it's gone. Hopefully she left it behind in Bungay, but she may have brought it here for that meeting with Professor Smiley. I'll tell you what, let's go into the building and find Cyril."

"Richard, what if she didn't go into the building? What if she's been abducted?"

"Let's not get melodramatic, that's the way your sister talks."

"Yes, but it's my sister we're talking about. You know how gullible she can be."

"Look, this is a very open area. I can't see anyone risking a disturbance out here in full view of the building. Look at all those windows. It's much more likely that she went into the building and got talking to someone."

"But Cyril hasn't seen her. Surely, she'd go straight to his office. I'm sure she knows the way quite well."

"That's true. I tell you what, just to put your mind at rest, why don't you go into the building and find Cyril. She may be with him already. I'll wait here in case she comes back to her car."

There was a lobby at the entrance to the building and a large noticeboard on the left-hand wall. One of the notices leapt straight out at me because of the large, black letters, 'LOCK YOUR CAR'. The notice went on to inform readers that there had been several reports of thefts from unlocked vehicles in the car park recently.

Nobody took any notice of me when I went into the building. Presumably they were used to visitors wandering around. A sign indicated that the corridor on my left led to a laboratory. I would surely be asked my business if I went in there, so I turned and went along the corridor in the opposite direction. Name plates on glass panelled doors leading off the corridor indicated to whom or for what purpose the rooms were allocated. The one solid door was designated 'Housekeeping'.

Was it my imagination or did I hear a scuffling coming from that room? I paused to listen. Could it be Gabriella locked inside? Just then, I heard footsteps approaching from round the corner. There was nowhere for me to hide, though looking back there was no reason for me to hide at all. Anyway, I turned and faced away from the direction of the oncoming footsteps, holding my breath, hoping not to be noticed. I needn't have bothered. The two people who walked past, deep in conversation, didn't even glance in my direction.

The muffled scuffling coming from the room marked 'Housekeeping' continued. I tried the door handle in fear and trepidation. To my surprise the room was unlocked. Still fearful, I opened the door wide. A large, well fed ginger cat leapt out and stalked past me with its tail in the air.

The encounter with the ginger cat brought me back to reality. With restored confidence I did what I should have done in the first place. I knocked on the door of the nearest room and asked for directions to Cyril's office.

29

The raised voices became louder as I approached Cyril's office. I could see through the glass panel on the door that there was someone in with him and he was shouting. There was no mistaking his voice even at that decibel level. I hesitated to knock on the door because I didn't think I should interrupt an argument with one of his colleagues. I tiptoed closer to the door and peered through the glass to see who the other person was. Surprise, surprise, it was none other than my missing sister. Mild, easy-going Cyril and happy go lucky Gabriella were going head-to-head in what might euphemistically be called a heated exchange.

I decided to give them a few minutes to settle down and moved a little way along the corridor to call Richard with the news that Gabriella was safe. I added that they were in the middle of one enormous row, and I thought it best not to interrupt. Richard took a more practical view of the situation.

"Never mind that, they'll get over it. Just go right in and ask your sister whether she left her data in her car boot."

"Are you sure? They're still going at it hammer and tongs."

"Yes, it could be very important."

I knocked on Cyril's door. There was no response. The two of them were glaring at each other, red faced. I went in and touched my sister's arm.

"Gabs, this is important. Did you leave your research data in your car boot?"

The angry look on her face changed instantly to one of horror. "What? Oh Cyril! Cyril! Oh no, please no!"

Cyril's anger morphed seamlessly into genuine concern. "Gabby sweetheart, what's happened."

I intervened. "Richard and I came back because Cyril phoned to ask if we knew where you were, Gabs. He was very worried because you hadn't turned up here."

She had the grace to look guilty. We could get to the bottom of that later.

"Gabs, your car boot lid was up and your clothes and things in a heap. We didn't see any boxes with your research material in them so…"

"Come on, Cyril!"

The two of them turned tail and ran out to the car park where Richard was waiting by the open boot. I followed.

Gabriella was the first to arrive. She made a beeline for the detergent and porridge boxes then flung her arms round Cyril's neck, whispering to him. Richard and I waited patiently while she sobbed quietly on his shoulder.

Cyril looked up at Richard, smiled and nodded. Richard pointed to the detergent and porridge boxes and asked, "Whose brainwave was it to use those particular boxes?"

Gabriella looked up from Cyril's shoulder. "Naturally we'd have used better boxes if there had been any available to us in your house. Honestly, Richard, Aggie never bothers to save useful boxes or string or brown paper."

"Well, just be glad she doesn't," Richard said heartily. "Those boxes fooled us and for all we know, may have fooled someone else this morning."

I quickly suggested we all go out for lunch. There had been enough misunderstanding and misinterpretation for one day.

Over lunch we learned what had happened. Cyril, we were told, had never driven Gabriel's Audi and wanted to try it out. That morning, he suggested that he should drive it straight to the Institute and make a start on work that had accumulated during his unplanned absence. Gabriella could drive Richard's car to our hotel and spend the morning with us, then we could all meet up for lunch.

Gabriella, who is the only person allowed to drive her car, nixed the idea immediately and told Cyril that no, she would take the Audi and he could return Richard's car *en route* to his office. She advised him, rather curtly, to set off early from Bungay so as to avoid the worst of the traffic. She would follow a little later in the Audi because she had to pack clothes and a few other bits and pieces she would need in Cambridge. She would catch up with him at the department. Their parting was unusually cool.

Cyril was really disappointed not to be allowed to take the Audi. Furthermore, he was not accustomed to being told what to do. He had not expected this from Gabriella. He felt let down. He ruminated all the way to work.

Gabriella on the other hand has always been bossy and saw nothing wrong with her alternative plan. She was surprised when his farewell that morning was less fond than usual. It only dawned on her after he left for Cambridge that she was possibly to blame and admitted to herself that she might have been more generous, or at the very least, countered his suggestion more gently.

This weighed increasingly on her mind as she drove to Cambridge. By the time she arrived at the Institute she had worked herself up into a veritable lather of remorse. She found it difficult to look cheerful and respond normally to us when we met her at the car park.

Walking from her car to the building, Gabriella's uneasiness increased. She felt too unsettled to go straight to Cyril's office. Instead, she decided to browse in the department library until she recovered her composure and felt more able to face him. A notice by the library door reminded her to switch off her mobile. She switched off and settled down to read some of the magazines. After half an hour's immersion in some very interesting articles, she felt sufficiently recovered. She availed herself of the facilities to wash her face and tidy her hair. For good measure she put on a little make-up — something she rarely bothered to do. Confidence restored, she sallied forth to Cyril's office.

Cyril, meanwhile, found he didn't have much work to catch up on after all and finished quickly. This gave him time to reflect on his earlier rattiness. They had never seriously disagreed on anything before, and he was anticipating her arrival somewhat nervously after that unusually cool parting.

As time went on and she didn't arrive his nervousness increased. He knew he had been a bit brusque before setting off from Bungay in Richard's car, but surely that wasn't enough to warrant keeping him waiting deliberately. He estimated she should have arrived at least half an hour ago. His first thought was that she had been held up somewhere, but in that case, why hadn't she phoned to let him know she'd be late? Then he worried that she could have been involved in an accident. She was not picking up his calls and he became increasingly anxious. He wished he had been nicer to her. That was when he called me to see if I had heard anything of her.

He just couldn't believe it when a smiling Gabriella suddenly appeared at his office, freshly made up and apparently not in any distress at all. Did she not realise the torment he had been in, imagining something terrible must have happened to her?

Before she had time to offer any explanation, he blurted out, "Where have you been?"

"In the library."

Cyril was too distressed to notice she was close to tears. His normally gentle voice increased in decibels with each word.

"In the library! In the library! You're telling me you've been in the library all this time!"

"Cyril I…"

"How could you? I've been worried sick wondering where you were! Why didn't you answer my calls?"

"Did you call me?"

"Yes, several times, and you didn't bother to answer!"

"Well, I didn't hear any calls."

"Don't be obtuse! How could you not hear your phone ring?"

"Well how could I hear? My phone was switched off."

"Why?"

"Because I was in the library. There's a notice that says…"

The drama ended when I walked into Cyril's office. The news of the open car boot brought it to a timely end.

30

After lunch with Richard and me, the two of them went off to Cyril's house, where they planned to stay until after the meeting with Professor Smiley. We went for another stroll along the banks of the River Cam, watching the punters ply their long poles. We hadn't got very far when Gabriella phoned.

"Hi, Aggie!"

"Hi! I guess you've been checking your data files. Were they all there in the boxes?"

"Yes, they're all there, but that's not what I'm calling you about, at least, not directly. It's like this, Aggie. Cyril and I have been discussing where they should be kept for safety in future. I'm all for keeping them in my house in Bungay, because lightning doesn't strike twice in the same place. Cyril isn't so sure. He says that if we're going to be living in Cambridge, it would be difficult to keep a very close eye on them because Bungay is almost a two-hour drive away, so I should bring all my stuff to Cambridge."

"That makes sense."

"Yes, Aggie, it makes sense if we decide to live in Cambridge, but I think we should live in Bungay. Frankly, I'm not overly impressed with Cyril's house. It redefines the term 'bachelor pad' with its spartan rooms and small garden. I just can't see us living there."

"Have you told Cyril this?

"Well, the thing is, Aggie, since that awful spat with him this morning, I've been thinking. Cyril is much more sensitive than I thought — in a good way of course. Anyway, I'm determined to be more thoughtful in future."

Promises, promises! I thought. I've heard that before.

"So, have you and Cyril come to any decision?"

"I told him I'd ask your opinion. I said you're a bit of a know-all but sometimes you can come up with quite good ideas. I was playing for time you see. I don't really expect you to be much help."

So much for her intention to be more thoughtful! I didn't remind her of it though because I wanted to continue the conversation.

"What did he say?"

"He grinned and said he couldn't wait to hear what good ideas the know-all comes up with."

The answer to Gabriella's dilemma was of course crystal clear to anyone looking at matter objectively, which she wasn't. I know my twin though. She always did resent advice from her elder sister, so I had to be diplomatic. I prefaced my remarks carefully.

"You don't have to take my advice of course, Gabs."

"Don't worry, I can judge whether it's good advice or not. No offence Aggie, but you're not always right. Remember..."

I cut her off. "Let's get back to the problem. You want to continue your work on compost and to keep your records safe, so you obviously have to live where you work. Cyril holds a senior position at the Institute and needs to live somewhere with a reasonable commute to his work. Now I take it that you and Cyril living separately is not an option."

"Aggie! We're getting married. Remember, we thought of doing it at Gretna Green. Of course we'll be living together."

"What about Cyril getting to work if you stay at Bungay?"

"Well, we'd have to work that out of course. Maybe he could work from home part of the time."

"At Bungay?"

"Well, yes. You know very well that I do all my work at Bungay."

"And what about the days Cyril needs to go to Cambridge?"

"Well yes, I suppose it is a bit of a drive."

"My opinion for what it's worth Gabs, is that you and Cyril should both sell up and put the proceeds into another place that suits both of you. Cyril needs to get to work, and you need a good-sized garden."

"I've already thought of that."

"Then why ask me?"

"Because I value your opinion."

She had neither thought it through nor valued my opinion, but I let it pass.

31

The matter was unexpectedly settled for Gabriella and Cyril at the meeting with Professor Smiley on the following day. Robert Carlisle, the head of research at a fertiliser company, had attended Professor Smiley's lecture. He had followed up on the exceptional degree of interest in Gabriella's composting success, shown by the audience, and contacted the Professor to discuss the matter. They agreed that while there was a lot of interest in Gabriella's work from amateur gardeners, there were no immediate prospect of developing her work commercially. Nevertheless, her findings identified interesting avenues for further research, which Robert Carlisle thought his firm would be prepared to sponsor. The purpose of the meeting therefore was specifically to sound out the extent of Gabriella's willingness to co-operate in identifying likely leads and to help plan, implement and coordinate multiple studies in universities across the UK.

This was put to Gabriella at the meeting. It was beyond her wildest dreams. All she could reply was, "Goodness, gracious!"

"What about you, Jenkinson?" asked Professor Smiley. "Would you be prepared to hold Dr Chester's hand for, say, the next five years?"

"I hope a lot longer than five years sir. I should tell you that Dr Chester has consented to be my wife."

"I wondered if there was some kind of relationship between you," said the Professor, "when I heard all that racket coming from your office yesterday."

"I can assure you sir," Cyril replied hastily, "that Gabriella, that is Dr Chester, and I could work very well together. I've seen the results of her composting experiments and it's my opinion that she has reached the stage where multiple larger scale trials under different conditions would be appropriate. If she's willing to go ahead, then so am I."

Gabriella, having by this time recovered her usual composure and confidence, affirmed her willingness.

"There's one thing I should point out, Professor Smiley," she said. "I'm not a member of the faculty here. If I'm to play a major role in this project, as I hope you're suggesting, I'll need either an official position within the department or recognised consultant status to give me the necessary authority."

"Indeed, you will. I think we can arrange something, an honorary fellowship maybe or certainly an official consultant position."

Robert Carlisle nodded his approval, then turned to Michael.

"We should thank Mr Winter too. If he hadn't left a message with my secretary about your lecture, Dr Smiley, I would not have known how much interest home gardeners take in Dr Chester's work."

Michael Winters had not said a word throughout the meeting. He now addressed Professor Smiley.

"Sir, this proposal to test the effectiveness of compost variations across the country is ingenious and exciting, but as you know, my main interest is in development and improvement of polytunnel techniques. Depending on the outcome of the study, there could be a valuable link with my work in the future. However, that would be, as you indicate, a few years down the line."

The Professor smiled. "Thank you, Mr Winter, I invited you to this meeting because you previously showed interest in Dr Chester's work. Let's not lose sight of the potential connection with polytunnel growing as the work progresses."

Michael Winter rose, "Thank you sir, and good luck with your research, Dr Chester." He smiled weakly, nodded to Gabriella and Cyril and left the room.

Robert Carlisle, Professor Smiley, Gabriella and Cyril stayed in the conference room to discuss the project in more detail. They did not see the two police officers waiting in the car park to put Michael in handcuffs as soon as he stepped out of the building. Jason Taylor had taken Cyril's advice to go to the police himself before they caught up with him. He admitted his own part in the two Bungay break-ins, and received a reduced sentence for naming Michael as the ringleader and agreeing to testify against him at trial.

EPILOGUE

Gabriella and Cyril did sell their houses and settled in a former farmhouse with a couple of acres outside Cambridge. That suited Gabriella's purposes, literally down to the ground. Other farm buildings were converted into office space for planning and subsequent administration of the compost research project. That, in turn, suited Cyril and the team of researchers seconded from the Institute.

Gabriella's son, George, had known nothing previously of his mother's association with Cyril, and had been out of the country on assignment since he lent us the BMW to drive to Scotland. None of us, not even his mother had thought to keep him up to date with the unfolding horticultural and romantic developments back home.

It was therefore a great shock, on his return, and learn that she planned on getting married again. And, as if marrying someone he had never met wasn't enough, she was moving to a new house, and undertaking a major role in what he crossly called 'PROJECT MUCK'. He was worried that she had taken on too much.

"At her age!", he growled to me just before the wedding.

"Now George," Richard said, "You didn't say that about your Aunt Aggie last year, when she married me and she's even older than your mother."

I put my arm round George's waist.

"It'll be your turn next, George."

And it was. And quite a story too!